Dark Dreams

John W. Smith

This book is manufactured in the United States.

This is a work of fiction; names, characters, places, and incidents are the product of the author's imagination, or are used fictitiously. Any resemblance to actual persons, living or dead, is entirely coincidental.

Copyright © 2015 John W. Smith

No parts of this book may be reproduced in any form or by any electric or mechanical means including photocopying, recording or by information retrieval and retrieval systems, without permission in writing from the publisher, in the case of brief quotations contained in critical articles and reviews.

Published in the United States by Well Read Press

All rights reserved.

Hard Cover ISBN: 978-0-9891810-3-7
Soft Cover ISBN: 978-0-9891810-4-4
Library of Congress: 2015939465

FIRST EDITION

Publisher:
Well Read Press
12545 State Route 143, Suite C #128
Highland, Illinois 62249

John W. Smith
Nightmares of a Mad Man
A Dark and Stormy Night, and anthology
Spirit Dagger, a Kindle short story
Colonial Scum, a Kindle short story
Hungry Things, a Kindle short story

WORDS OF PRAISE

John Smith's skewed visions make for an entertaining mix of suspense, humor, and fear blended with quirky twists that slip you into the story and hold you there. These imaginings could only come from a warped mind that doesn't just bend reality, but turns sharp corners into a deep, dark realm and laughs at the absurdities slinking from shadow to shadow.

The variety is refreshing; his tales run the gambit from vampires and werewolves to world decimating computers, knights and dragons, even romance. Nothing is sacred.

I love the author's smooth, no nonsense writing style that keeps the story moving with good pacing and just enough detail to allow the reader's imagination to run free. Admittedly, his dialogue can get a little hokey at times, but that just adds to the humor. His unveiling of the characters within their worlds has you standing beside them throughout their experiences rather than watching from the sidelines. You can feel the heat of the fire and smell the blood of the heart still pumping in your hand.

To him, the mind is a playpen and emotions are Tinker Toys. He dips your toes into the shadow world, as if testing the waters, before dunking you into the inky black pool.

I have read all of John Smith's works and have never been disappointed. He excels at "getting you in the end."

Though this is a collection of short stories, you'll want to keep turning the pages just to see what he's come up with next.

Sandra Maue - author of *Cardiac Arrest, A Perfect Storm (A Dark and Stormy Night anthology),* and *The Flip-Flop Debacle*

John has come a long way as a writer. I met him while working at the *Bakersfield Californian*. He wrote crisp, concise sentences in the advertising department. At the time, he was in the Air Force Reserve and wrote a variety of feature stories and news about his unit. His work was informative and interesting. He has grown as a writer, being more descriptive and telling creative tales. John prides himself in leaving a lot of details to the mind of the reader; I tend to be very descriptive and leave no questions to the stories.

In *Dark Dreams,* what is most appealing is how, like in his stories, our life experiences can start in the same place but end up in different places. Let's look at three examples from this book.

Who among us has been angered or harmed by someone and thought, *I could kill you?* We say the words but don't mean them, we don't plan it and never act on the thought. That is why John's story, "Tooth Fairy," appeals to me. Our main character stumbles onto a tooth fairy and offers her ideas to help meet her collection goal. Her response requires no thought or causation, simply an action that meets her needs but leaves no quarter under my pillow at the end of the story.

I had a similar reaction when reading "Speaking of Black Holes." The story works for me. The principle character literally sticks it to the man, the government and all those who blindly follow orders from people who have no idea what reactions their decisions hold for the multitudes.

I found "Treasure Hunt" enjoyable on many levels. Primarily, the story shows that the best laid plans often fall short of the intended goal. There is solid historical backbone in the story involving ancient South American societies and a modern treasure hunter.

I highly recommend Dark Dreams to anyone who willing to explore the darker side of life and wonders exactly when truth becomes fiction.

Jaime R. (Jim) Cancio
Author of *Once Upon a Time*

John Smith has exposed many people's paranoia. His deeply ironic tale of Red Dawn" coming to life, in his story "Paranoia Runs Deep" is like an episode of the *Twilight Zone;* the story gradually sucks you in with a cruel practical joke and then slams your senses with an unexpected ending that leaves you dangling and not knowing if the nightmare is real or not. He achieves maximum irony with minimum words. "Tooth Fairy" is a darkly humorous short story guaranteed to leave the reader snickering in delight. It is a sly, diabolical black comedy worthy of the *Outer Limits.*

"Living Doll" is a darkly entertaining tale of an elegantly evil doll who would terrify Chuckie into submission and have him saying, "Yes, dear" in a meek little voice. Elizabeth, the doll, would bring him to his knees. From her first appearance as a gift fit for a delightful daughter, the doll is the center of an unearthly plot and would fit in nicely as a minion of demonic malice in *Sleepy Hollow*. The not-unexpected ending will leave you shaking your head and wondering what is next.

John has a truly diabolical sense of humor, which makes his writing all the more enjoyable because of its inherent charm.

Elle Nyman
Contributor to Midwest Outdoors Magazine and several newspapers.

John Smith manages to go deep into the vault filled with your worst nightmares in his latest book, *Dark Dreams*, bringing you face-to-face with all that may be waiting or lurking in the dark. From turning a beloved childhood icon into something to fear, to questioning what happens when mankind's wealth of knowledge becomes more of a danger than a blessing, Mr. Smith sets the stage for our worst nightmares to come to life. So, turn on all the lights, pull up the covers, get comfortable in your bed and start reading, but be forewarned, Smith's vivid tales of woe will leave you wondering if it's safe to turn out the lights and close your eyes. Or... if *Dark Dreams* will visit you tonight!

Kat Perry
Author of *"The Calm," "Death Becomes Her Lover"*

The stories John Smith pens in this book of short stories show an imagination that knows no bounds. The reader never finds comfort in knowing where the story is going or where it will end. Whether writing about good Samaritans, criminals, fairies, vampires, or clones, the characters refuse to conform to expectations. Though his narrative often centers on the darker aspects of storytelling, John Smith approaches that darkness with a subtle hand, often not fully realized until the closing passages of the tale. It is this approach to his craft that keeps the reader engaged and the pages turning until the end.

Mark Laramore,
Author of "Storm Nebula," from the anthology, *A Dark and Stormy Night*

DEDICATION

This book is dedicated to everyone who has ever had a nightmare, bad dream, thoughts or idea that popped into your mind while trying to sleep. This book demonstrates that many of us have similar dreams, light and happy as well as dark and frightening.

May all your dreams bring you resolution to problems that allow you to rise in the morning with a smile.

ACKNOWLEDGEMENTS

This book is dedicated to all the people in the four writers' groups who listened to the stories and offered constructive ideas to help them flow and, in some cases, actually make sense. I also want to thank Jim Cancio, Kat Perry and JoAnn Bockenfeld who reviewed the stories and searched for errors in punctuation, grammar, spelling and all the other little mistakes, which can turn a good book into the best book it can become.

Thank you to Lori Perkins and her team at Absolute Publishing Services for taking the manuscript and turning it into a high quality book.

Last, but not least, a special thank you to my mom who allowed me to spend hours, days and weeks hunched over the computer keyboard, creating and editing this work.

Thank you, the readers, for purchasing this book and making it more than just therapy writing. I hope you enjoy the stories.

A special thank you to my mom who allowed me to spend hours, days and weeks hunched over the computer key board creating and editing this work

AUTHORS COMMENTS

Dark Dreams is not a sequel to my first book of short stories, *Nightmares of a Mad Man*. I admit that most of the stories take an unexpected turn at the end. I have read and been told by others far more successful than me that in order to be recognized, a writer needs to publish three books in the same genre. Thanks to my coordinating and editing *A Dark and Stormy Night, an anthology,* this book meets my goal of writing in the vein of Rod Serling and the variety of television shows following his success.

I will continue writing dark fiction and horror, but I have been challenged to turn my writing 180 degrees in another direction by writing a romantic novel. I have been thinking of various storylines and characters for the past two years. It is now time to settle down and develop a story that any mother would enjoy, include an ending where the couple lives happily ever after. Of course, I wonder, will they be human, robotic or an alien race living undetected on Earth? Only time will tell.

TABLE OF CONTENTS

Paranoia Runs Deep...1
A Taste of Silence...7
Summation...15
Blood on the Dance Floor..21
Fun House..27
Tooth Fairy..33
Living Doll...35
You Want It … You Got It..41
A Night on the Couch..49
Dark Window..55
Open All Night… Donors Welcome....................................63
Follow That Man..71
Electronic Terrorist..77
Resolution..85
Castle of Night … Vindication..91
Speaking of Black Holes..101
Treasure Hunt...111
About The Author..121

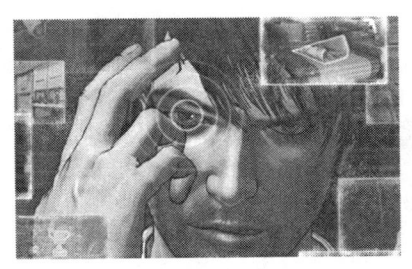

Paranoia Runs Deep

"I'm telling you man. The government is tracking us. They've already taken over Gmail©, Yahoo©, Google© and YouTube©. In addition, they monitor our telephone calls, check our tweets, and the new televisions and computers with cameras can spy on us in our homes. There is no such thing as privacy anymore.

"The U.N. has hidden bases throughout the states and on command will march in and take over our cities. They are using foreign armies because they know that our soldiers will join us," Ralph ranted. "This nation belongs to a conglomerate of foreign powers."

Every week, Ralph, Billy, Mark, and I would meet for coffee and discuss our current writing. Unfortunately, Ralph had a new rant each week. The topic cycled from various black caverns of his mind. There was nothing pleasant, always doom and gloom, end of the world thoughts that would haunt him until he obsessed on a new subject.

I remember Ralph's paranoia at the turn of the century. He was focused for months on the end of the world as we knew it; Y2K meant there would be no water, power or food. Gangs of people would be going from house to house pillaging, plundering, raping and killing. The search for food, guns and water was always the common thread. Poor Ralph designed a safe route out of town, to be taken after dark on New Year's Eve.

When Christmas arrived, he had convinced himself that all was lost. His bunker created, he had stockpiled all necessary supplies, as well as arms and ammunition that would allow us to protect ourselves from people trying to escape the destruction of the city and take our sanctuary, eat our food and, of course, kill us.

Naturally, I voted that we keep all small children for food and a limited number of women for servants; after all, someone had to cook the meals and keep us warm at night.

Ralph would give me dirty looks; however, he didn't object to the idea. He told his merry band of followers how he disassembled several weapons and hid them in various areas within his truck. He advised us to do the same because the police and army would search all vehicles on the road after everything shut down. He gave us the secret light blink and horn signal so he wouldn't shoot us as we entered the compound.

Unfortunately, Ralph was the only person to hide in the mountains. He missed the great party as 1999 became history and 2000 brought no changes in modern society.

After January had come to an end, Ralph continued his obsession, "We need to prepare, fall off the grid and be ready to make our escape by the back roads when those Chinese troops spread out in every city and start shooting everyone in sight."

"What makes you think the U.N. troops are Chinese?" Billy asked as he winked to the rest of us.

"God, that is simple. First they own this country; they bought it from the Japanese, you know. Second they hate us and third they want our resources. What those idiots in Washington don't realize is political correctness will be the death of our way of government and that the leaders will be the first to be executed."

Ralph explained how the liberal media was in on the plot. "They will tell everyone the takeover is appropriate, that we can't control crime and this is for the good of the country. We will lose our civil liberties and there will be no Bill of Rights. Anyone who disagrees with them will be arrested or shot."

"They are going to have problems taking over the cities," Mark chimed in. "The gangs and bikers will kick their asses."

"Not for long," Ralph countered. "These guys will have assault weapons, grenades, rocket launchers and it won't take long for their aircraft to take out pockets of resistance. My guess is they already have planes sitting on abandoned airfields ready to strike when all this goes down. After all, they won't be worried about collateral damage of homes and people.

"Military commanders will be ordered not to release weapons to our troops to help defend the citizens and within five days the country we love to hate will be no more."

Billy, who loved to mess with everyone's mind, looked at Ralph and said in his most serious voice, "How will you know when they are ready to strike?"

Ralph's eyes gleamed; he had converted one of us. "Easy ... Men in black suits and sunglasses will start showing up at homes, business and hang outs. People will be forced into their vans, never to be seen again. They will take people who disagree with the government or express different views; people with weapons, anyone they feel would be a threat to their plans. I'm sure they have lists of people and addresses they will want to eliminate before the assault takes place."

"Ah," said Billy, "You mean the people Homeland Security monitors and trouble-makers the FBI have on their lists as potential threats. I imagine the CIA has names of potential traitors; the number of people that begin to disappear should alert the government or someone that the country is being invaded.

"All the spying the NSA has been caught doing will expand the list. They use that big computer and spy on all emails, telephone conversations, tweets, Face Book® comments and even cards and letters. The post office gets monitored.

"These people will be prioritized as the first to go, followed by secondary threats, my guess the conservative media, and then the attack will be initiated. We have to keep a lookout for stories about these things happening so we can head to Canada or Mexico before it's too late."

"Exactly!" Ralph exclaimed.

"Brother, you are in a heap of shit," Mark stated quietly. "As far as I'm concerned, you would be public enemy number one in this town."

The color drained from Ralph's face. "What ... What do you mean? I can't be a public enemy. I'm going off the grid!"

"Unless you're packed and plan on moving now, they probably know you better than you know yourself. Let me start at the top. Are you not the man writing to three women in China and other countries concerning their coming to America to be your wife?"

Ralph nodded.

"Are you not the man who on three occasions has been taken to court due to supposed threats to individuals of various national origins?"

Again Ralph nodded.

"Have you not been ordered by judges to get rid of your guns and, because you talk too much, got several other people in trouble because they were holding handguns and rifles for you?"

Ralph's eyes began to tear. "Yes," he whispered.

"And last but not least, are you not the man who always talks about the shootouts you have had with robbers and gang members when you worked at a convenience chain and other businesses, plus at one time had a swat team surrounding your home and you told them you were cleaning your guns while watching a movie and wouldn't come out until the movie ended?"

Ralph slumped in his chair. "Guilty."

I brought myself into the conversation, "Ralph, aren't you always sending emails concerning the evils of government and plots by the government to do away with constitutional law and replace it with Shia law?"

"Oh God," he whimpered as tears rolled down his cheek.

"I would say that the government, Home Land Security and the U.N. identified you a long time ago as a malcontent. You need to pack up and leave, and not just town, but the state, perhaps the country. You can't use debit or credit cards; cash can't be tracked. You must travel back roads and not break a single speed limit or run a stop sign. I'm not sure it would be safe to stay in a motel, especially if they post your picture on a wanted list. You must no longer exist."

Ralph looked at us in shock.

"Oh," I continued, "and you can't tell your girlfriends in China, England or anywhere else goodbye. Don't call friends or family; you will alert the government. Don't tell anyone you are leaving; they may tell the government when questioned. You must cease to exist. One comment to anyone and you are busted and picked up before you can make your move. Travel light, my friend, and travel now."

Billy, Mark and I gave a slight grin to one another. For once, Ralph had backed himself into a corner. He now had plenty to think about.

"Well, I've got to run," I said. "See you all next week. I'm tied up with work and will be out of town until Friday."

Mark and Billy stood to leave. Ralph remained sitting. He was shaking with fear and tears were running down his face. He looked like he had a wife, mistress and a house payment, all a month late. We dumped our trash and headed to our cars.

We were standing in the side parking lot laughing about how we had finely pulled one over on Ralph when we saw a large black van pull up to the door of the coffee shop. Three big men in black suits and sunglasses climbed out of the side door. They scanned the area and looked in the window. One of them nodded his head and an even bigger man got out. They checked the street. One agent headed down the alley to the back entrance.

The leader touched his ear and the three of them entered the coffee shop, one of them blocked the front door.

Mark and Billy looked at me. "Oh Shit," we said together. We moved and angled ourselves towards the back of the van that allowed us to see if they brought Ralph out dead or alive.

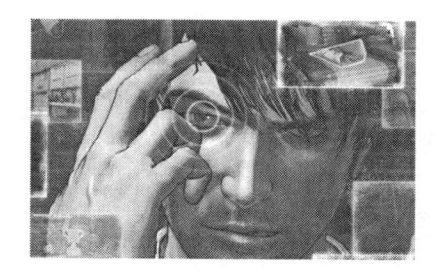

A Taste of Silence

He sat at the end of the bar head down, reading a book and ignoring those around him. It was happy hour, the time when people weary of their jobs and responsibilities filtered into the bar for a drink or ten before heading to a home and family that continued to push them deeper into the muck of life.

His little book light provided all he needed to read. The wine glass beside the book was half-full. The liquid rippled as loud music vibrated from the speakers, yet he seemed not to notice. The noise of conversation along the bar seemed to disappear before it reached his ears. He sat reading, wetting his finger in the wine before licking it and turning the page. In a world of noise and frustration, he was an island of calm, waiting for some new attraction to enter his space.

She entered and stopped just inside the door. The shock of light to dark and the beat of the music overwhelmed her. She felt dizzy. Closing her eyes, she took a few deep breaths and focused her thoughts, seeking some sort of asylum from the terrors outside and the chaos in the bar.

The sounds of the city faded until she no longer heard them. The desperate cries of people trying to rediscover joy shocked her system, but again, she focused on calm. Somewhere in the bar, he waited to bring her the peace she had sought since her recovery.

She removed her sunglasses, her eyes accustomed to the low light. She ignored the various flashing lights synced with the techno rock blasting from the DJ's speakers. After looking over all the tables, she searched the bar. She was amazed at the number of circular tables surrounded with desperate people unable to fill the holes in their empty lives. She ignored the dance floor with men and women bouncing and rubbing against one another, hoping to find the one person that would fill their hunger for pleasure and, in some cases, violence, at least for tonight.

She saw him reading at the far end of the bar. The music and human drama seeped back into her consciousness. She watched him for a few moments before stepping further in. She seemed to glide toward this silent dark stranger; drawn to him by some unknown magnetic force emanating from the music.

No one noticed her as she made her way toward the darkened corner. People moved out of her way without knowing she existed. She was within his arm's reach before hesitating. She had come so far, and now ... now she wasn't sure what to do next. One deep breath and she wedged herself between the reader and the sleeping drunk on the next stool. She stared into the mirror, studying him. She saw nothing special except that he was at peace with himself. He ignored her and everything around him.

He would dip his finger in the wine glass, lick it and then turn another page. She wasn't sure he was reading; his pace was constant. He ignored her as he focused on the book. She recognized the title in the mirror, but couldn't remember the story. All she remembered was the book was filled with sex and violence. It was one of those underground books where the writer and the reader lived the raw experiences of life. The story focused in minute detail on the evils mankind forces on itself. The stories were weak, but the people reading the books considered the works fine literature.

Watching him, she ordered and drank some sort of watered down clear soda; she wasn't going to dull her senses with alcohol. Her mind wandered as she stared at him and thought about the book. The two seemed worlds apart; then again, you can't tell a serial killer from the boy next door until he has the knife at your throat.

Her body jerked when she realized that their eyes were locked together. Her mouth went dry, her pulse increased and her face felt flushed as he focused on her. *Damn*, she thought *I should have been careful, stayed focused or sat at a table and watched him.* She turned, facing him with a small upturned lip that could have resembled a smile in other circumstances.

He studied her with his intense eyes. She felt as though he not only looked at her but saw through her clothing ... saw her naked. But she realized his stare was far stronger than a normal man's; she felt him look deep into her soul. He learned about her past and present. He knew her mission; why she stood silent before him.

He raised a hand and pointed with crossed fingers. The bartender brought her another drink, this one more of an amber color instead of clear soda. She took it without hesitation and raised it to her lips as he nodded his head. The liquid burned its way down her throat and emanated from her stomach to every nerve in her body.

He took the glass from her hand and pulled her closer to him. She felt her thighs against his body. He put his arm around her waist; she, in return, put hers across his shoulders.

"I assume this is supposed to be some sort of accident that we found each other tonight," he whispered.

A shiver consumed her body. Her legs felt like rubber. His arm around her waist steadied her. She regained her strength, refusing to break the eye contact between them.

Standing once again, she realized that he sat in an area of silence and now, she had joined him. She looked into the mirror. The bar was packed with people, heads and bodies moving to the beat of music. People were dancing, drinking and shouting as the music increased in volume; yet, within his circle, the wine did not vibrate from the noise and she could hear ... nothing.

He held up three fingers and another drink was placed before her. This drink was ruby red. He smiled at her. "This is different from the sludge the regulars drink," he said. "It will take the edge off your day but keep your mind clear."

The bartender turned and walked away. *He must have a tab. He didn't ask for money.* Again, she looked at the mirror. He smiled and nodded his head again. She felt as though he spoke to her without words. She raised the glass, swallowed and allowed the liquid to command her body.

The red had no kick, no burn, but within seconds, she felt calm and relaxed. This was a feeling she had never experienced in her adult life. She looked at him and smiled. The silence was growing on her. She loved it. She knew she had found one of the few people who could bring her peace.

He turned on his stool. With his right elbow on the bar, he studied her once again. This time, he appeared to be a man appreciating the looks of an elegant woman or a painting or a horse -- something to be owned, not loved or cared for.

She stepped between his legs, snuggling to him as close as possible. *If he wants to look, let him feed his hunger. He has what I need and I'm going to get it.*

He propped his legs on the bottom rung of the stool. For the first time he spoke. "Sit, make yourself comfortable."

The sleeping drunk was still on the other stool; it took her a second before she realized that he intended she sit on his knee. Carefully, she slid on his lap. She had to admit, it felt good to get off her feet. The six inch heels weren't made for walking or standing for long.

"So tell me, little one," his voice was smooth and hypnotic, "Why have you sought me out?"

She watched him for several seconds. He had made no attempt to caress her legs or touch her breasts. He kept his hand around her waist for balance. She felt secure. He would do nothing unexpected to frighten her. She needed to tell him her problem and ask him for the cure.

She attempted to speak but no sound came out. She couldn't understand what had happened. She began to panic but his voice, once again, put her at ease.

"This is a place of silence; do not interrupt the flow of peace and well-being. There is no talking; all you need to do think."

She realized his lips were not moving. She looked around once again and realized that the real world surrounded them but was not allowed to invade their space. This was exactly what she needed: solitude.

Her mind raced as she told him her story. Sometimes she looked him in the eyes, other times she stared at him and the world around them in the mirror. She told him of the accident and the coma when she was eighteen. She shouldn't have lived, but when they disconnected her life support, she woke and recovered. She hated being alive.

She explained her sensitivity to sight and sound. Normal conversations were shouts, shouts were explosions. The thoughts of people battered against her body non-stop.

She explained how she learned meditation and other forms of mind and body control just to survive the day. Her respite was brief and never complete, until now ... until this very moment.

He smiled as he raised his finger once again. The bartender brought two glasses of something deep green. It looked emerald as he set it on the dark oak bar. He tilted his head in question. She smiled and nodded yes. Her hand wrapped around the glass as though reaching for a lifeline.

He studied her again. "You are sure this is what you want?" he asked as he slid his arms around her waist. "You wish to give up your gift rather than learn to control it? You seek eternal rest over life?"

She took one hand and held it to his cheek. "Yes, please yes," she pleaded. "Peace of mind. I'll do anything; give up everything if I can experience the never ending peace and silence."

The man became serious, "Would you be willing to give up your powers rather than live in this world?" he asked one last time.

The woman let go of the glass and hugged him. She sobbed, "Please take it away. I thought you were a legend, a myth, but I have found you. I must have freedom. I can no longer live in this chaos."

The man sighed. He squared his shoulders. He acknowledged her mission and decided to grant her request. "Straddle me," he commanded.

She stood and placed her legs outside both of his in a lovers' embrace. She leaned into him as he leaned back on the stool. Had they not been dressed, she would have felt embarrassed. Staring into the mirror, she again realized that no one in the bar paid any attention. Only the bartender acknowledged their presence.

Her skirt rode high on her thighs; she felt him grow. He released himself and pushed into her body. Handing her the newest drink, they toasted. There was no sound as the glasses clinked. They consumed the drink as newlyweds drinking from the other's glass.

She felt strange. Her body tingled as the liquid spread throughout her. Her mind seemed to float to some unknown world with strange figures dancing in the woods. Once solid, she watched herself fade from this world.

He smiled as he sat down his glass. She seemed frozen in time, unmoving and staring like a statue into his eyes.

"My dear, you are a Solitary Fairy. A very old Solitary Fairy. Somehow, you managed to adapt to the ways of humans. I can see you moving from place to place every few years, holding a variety of jobs, never knowing why you didn't seem to age as fast as those around you. The crowds and the noise you find in your mind are reflections of your past. Your life belongs to the forest and the solitude found away from humanity."

She whispered, "Yes," as she felt herself soaking into his being. His power surrounded her, relieving all her stress and cares.

"You were involved in an accident; you were on a train that

came off the tracks. You remembered nothing of your past. Because of the damage to your mind, you did not gain any powers until later in life. Now, you are mature and have reacquired some of your fairy talents. You failed to control the talents and now those talents are trying to escape the captivity of your human existence.

"Thanks to Mankind, there are no fairies to help you control the powers as there were when you were young. It will be impossible for you to explore your powers here in the city; you need the countryside to experiment and return to your full greatness. You are still young and can achieve great power, if you are willing."

She listened to his words as she looked into the mirror; she appeared opaque. She could see through herself. Small spots of light circled around her. She realized she was seeping into him; she was dissolving and becoming a part of his existence. Frightened, she wanted to push away, but he held her tight.

She watched the colors of the drinks floating inside her. She felt them turning her into some kind of sack. It didn't make sense; she was dissolving into liquid. She turned her head and looked deep into his eyes.

"Had you learned to control your power or had in this instant wished to learn the ways of your kind, I would have taken you under my wing and trained you to become a powerful queen and my thrall. You are, or, should I say, were a ten thousand year old princess centuries ago when I first tasted you. The power you would possess now would be limitless."

He brought her face closer to his, "That link is how you found me, and it is through that link I will provide the freedom you seek." His hands embraced her face as their lips met in a kiss. "You taste as sweet as you did all those millennia ago," he whispered.

She felt secure as their lips met. Seconds later, her memories returned. She was more than a princess even then. She was the Solitary Fairy Queen, ruler of all the Emerald Isles. She was fair, but harsh, until men ceased to believe in magic. The kiss took her powers and control.

After the accident, she saw her life as human and now as something indescribable. She grew tired as the kiss continued. She didn't understand or care. She was at peace, eternal peace as his embrace and kiss grew tighter with growing passion. He ended the kiss. The last of her will dissolved. She resisted nothing as he stroked her pliable body, turned her head and buried his fangs into her neck.

Slowly, she disappeared, her entire being sucked from her body to his. There was nothing left but what appeared to be a thin plastic container. The last of the sparkling liquid consumed, he tossed the skin on the bar.

The bartender came to claim the skin. "Too bad," he whispered, "She was quite a looker and, from her reactions coming in, quite powerful."

He smiled. "Yes, all true. She was a powerful drink. And as we both know, the best tasting drink for a vampire is Fairy blood."

The bartender chuckled as he walked away with the skin. The old man returned to his book.

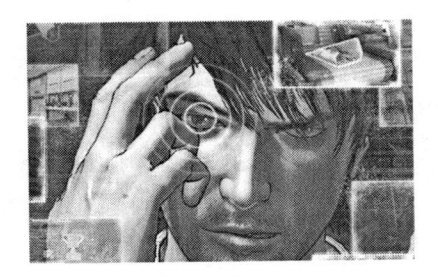

Summation

It had been a long and drawn out trial. Both sides had taken their time in jury selection. As the defense attorney, I felt sorry for Juror Number One as she sat through an additional four weeks of potentials until the panel and alternates were chosen.

Thanks to the publicity, the jury was sequestered in a hotel near the courthouse. Television service in their rooms had been terminated. Newspapers, magazines, cell phones and other forms of communication were not allowed. The judge wanted to keep outside influences from affecting the verdict.

Jurors were not allowed to go to the newsstand to buy snacks, gum or soft drinks without an escort. The judge assigned deputies to monitor every action when out of their rooms. The telephone service was turned off. Calls home were allowed once a day. All calls were placed on a speaker phone and under the supervision of a U.S. Marshal.

The trial itself had taken eight months. The prosecution spent over six months bringing forth witnesses against my client. Most of the testimony was hearsay, much of it thrown out of court and the jury told to disregard it, but everyone knew the jury wouldn't forget. My client was hated.

My defense concentrated on cross examination of the prosecution witnesses and the examination of the few people willing to testify as to the character of my client. A logical person would have dismissed all charges and set my client free. But, these were not logical times, and the trial seemed to drag into eternity.

The length of this legal circus had caused marital problems. The spouses of two of the jurors started ongoing affairs, and made no secret about their activities as they attended the trial holding hands, and wrapping their arms around each other. They enjoyed flaunting these activities at their spouses. It was rumored the empanelled spouses more than got even in the hotel paid for by the state.

Another juror had lost parents in an accident and was unable to attend the funeral. Three others had lost their jobs due to their employers' inability to hold their positions since someone was needed to do their physical work.

All in all, my client took my advice and ignored the jury as their hate-filled stares charged the courtroom each day. My client sat in his chair, head down, ignoring the entire process. He refused to testify in his own defense.

He looked me straight in the eyes and said, "Why bother, they have made up their minds. They hate me. If God himself came down and testified for me, they would still find me guilty. I'm innocent, but they are going to fry me because they can."

The prosecution wrapped up his case. He spent the next week presenting his closing arguments. He summed up everything, and I mean everything. He even rehashed the evidence that had been thrown out. As he closed, all twelve members of the jury looked at my client. As he looked at the table, I observed every jury member's eyes -- the look of death stared down on both of us. The judge saw it but said nothing as he shared their hate. At that point, I knew he would get the maximum sentence: death. Everyone considered him guilty.

The prosecutor concluded with "Thank you for your attention and service to your community, I look forward to your verdict of guilty."

I rose from my seat. "Your honor, I would like to propose a recess until tomorrow. I believe everyone is tired and could use a break after the several days of summation."

The judge agreed. I had until tomorrow at ten a.m. to develop a closing statement that would put reasonable doubt in one -- and only one -- person's mind. A hung jury would give my client a second chance in a new trial.

The next morning, everyone stood as the judge entered the courtroom. Glaring at my client, he asked, "Are you ready to close, Mr. Defense Attorney?"

I knew I was in trouble when he couldn't even call me by name. The jury sat straight in their chairs, arms crossed. They challenged me to say anything that would change their minds.

"Your honor, members of the jury ... I hate pre-planning and pre-conceived notions; however, those concepts are not well received by prosecutors and juries in courts of law ... I feel it is my duty to not waste your time with days of a drawn out monolog refuting the prosecutor's entire summation of the evidence and misinformation thrown out during the trial. You were told to disregard over ninety-nine percent of what he had to say during the trial, so he chose to remind you of stories and half-truths during his summation.

"From the looks on your faces, I will assume he accomplished his task and you are prepared to give my client the maximum sentence for his charges. My summation will be short, spoken from the heart and from my observations of the accused.

"My client did not break any laws of the land. His refusal to testify was brought on by your looks and attitude toward him because of your inability to remain impartial. Every one of you has ignored his actions that brought him to this courtroom. You simply cling to your beliefs of the type of person -- yes person -- he has shown by his actions. He feels that his defense is a lost cause.

"I disagree. Let me sum the entire case in a few sentences. Without warning and preplanning, my client was innocently walking down the street; he heard screams coming from an alley and ran to investigate. This shows great courage; most people would have continued walking and ignored the call of someone in need. My client chose to take action and help a complete stranger.

"He found a man beaten beyond recognition, called 9-1-1 for help and stayed until authorities arrived. My client gave his statement to law enforcement and when dismissed by police, went on about his business. He was, however, unable to continue with his life when the investigation discovered that the beaten man, the man who died, was identified as my client.

"Everyone in this room knows that cloning a human has never been recorded and is illegal. This court knows that my client had no brothers and we have no idea if the person sitting before you is the original Alfred Jacobs, a freak of nature or a clone. For the record, no one can state that the victim in this case was the original Alfred Jacobs. My client has no other identity. There should have been no DNA match to my client and the deceased, but it matched perfectly. There are no logical explanations as to why both men shared the exact same DNA because it is impossible for two people to have the same DNA. My client knows he is the real Alfred Jacobs, a retail sales clerk who has never been in trouble his entire life.

"Then there is this other Alfred Jacobs, an assassin for hire, bank robber and the enforcer behind the most powerful crime family in this state. Was the Alfred Jacobs beaten in the alley the assassin or the clerk? Was he a clone or a joined twin separated at birth from his brother? Who is Alfred Jacobs and how did the two come together in one place? Was it by plan and purpose? ... Fate? ... Coincidence? ... Or unintended faithful synchronicity by person, place and situation? I'm afraid we will never know.

"I ask you to take a good look at my client. He lacks the inner strength to be a cold heartless assassin ... my client is a caring individual who has never thought of harming another living thing. He could not look at you, the jury, during this trial because it hurt him to see your hate. He is soft spoken and not coordinated. The guards have commented that he cringed at the other inmates in lock up, tripped over his own feet and stammered when confronted by his cell mates. This is not the personality of a cold blooded killer. He could not have killed the second Alfred Jacobs found in the alley.

"The evil Alfred Jacobs was beaten and died in the hospital and I ask you to consider, simply consider the possibility that before you sits an innocent man. Thank you."

The jury deliberated three hours. I knew my client would be found guilty. Everyone agreed the jury had arrived at the verdict too fast. The courtroom was filled; people stood in the halls. Television cameras lined up outside the courthouse; reporters filled the stairs and stood along the chamber walls. The trial of the century was coming to an end. Absolute attentive silence reigned throughout the courtroom, in the hallways and throughout the courthouse, even in the restrooms.

The judge looked at the stern faces of the jury. "Have you reached a verdict?" He asked.

"We have your honor," responded the foreman. With a nod from the judge, the foreman read, "On the first count, we, the jury, find the defendant, Alfred Jacobs, not guilty of the murder of Alfred Jacobs in the first degree. On the second count of multiple murders as an assassin, we find the defendant, Alfred Jacobs, not guilty."

There was a gasp from everyone in the courtroom. Reporters rushed out to contact their editors. The judge demanded order in his court.

"Is this a unanimous decision?" he asked the jury foreman.

She nodded. "Yes, sir. The jury agreed that there is reasonable doubt to convict Mr. Jacobs as there is no way to prove if he is the true individual, a clone or a killer."

Alfred released a long sigh. He smiled for the first time since we met over a year ago. He was in shock. He shook my hand and hugged me. "Thank you. I don't know how you did it, but thank you."

The judge banged his gavel once again, thanked the jury for their service and looked at Alfred with the hate that still filled his eyes. "Mr. Jacobs," he began, "the charges against you are hereby dismissed and you are free to go. But, be advised, you are now on my radar and law enforcement will be watching. If you are the assassin, you will find yourself back in my court and I can promise you that things will not go as well as they have today."

Alfred looked into the judge's eyes. "You won't see me again, Your Honor. It doesn't matter if I am the original or a copy, you have made me famous. I have made a mark on society and plan to promote the rights of all individuals, whether original or copied."

Alfred hugged me one last time and whispered in my ear, "You did well, Mr. Anderson. For someone who doesn't believe in pre-planning, that was a powerful summation. Of course, if you can make one clone, you can make many. Do not worry, your future is secure and thanks to the publicity, my others know what you have done. Live a long and happy life."

A few hours later, Alfred was released from lock up. His possessions in hand, he walked out of the courthouse basement with me. We shook hands and parted ways.

Crossing the street, Alfred was hit by a bus and killed. His fingerprints, photos, all records of his existence were taken out of the system and filed with other deceased criminals, accused and ordinary citizens. As far as the world was concerned, Alfred Jacobs no longer existed.

Three days later, I sat at a coffee shop looking out the window watching people. I saw Alfred walk past and look in. Smiling, he looked at me, gave a thumbs up for victory and walked on.

Five weeks later, I received a check for six million dollars from an obscure organization thanking me for assisting reproduced individuals worldwide. The note ended with "Consider this your payment for services and a retainer for future work. We will be in touch. Yours Truly, Alfred."

Blood on the Dance Floor

Detective Earl Vaughn stood and studied the far wall above the dance floor; there was a smattering of brain material and a lot of blood. From the looks of the splatter pattern, there was more blood than brains. He could distinguish the trail of brains to the wall. He had to admit, it was hard to tell where the brains ended and blood began since both had pooled and then dried together as gravity forced it to the floor. As he looked down, he discovered the bulk of the blood with no brains on display was pooled in the middle of the dance floor.

It had been there for months, possibly years. The blood had gone from bright red to the dried, almost dark maroon color found when it dries and, over time, turns to a reddish powder and is layered into and covered in several inches of dust and dirt. The body was shriveled; the lower extremities were a dark color tainted from pooled blood. As Vaughn slowly crossed the floor, he examined the thick layer of dust that held no foot prints or other indications of anyone being in the building for a long time. He remained at least five feet from the gore. It was an old crime scene, but there was no reason to ruin potential evidence.

The CSI team arrived several minutes behind him. They stopped beside him and stared, "Holy Shit," muttered one of them, "Why were we called out? That body is so old it could be my great-grandma."

Vaughn turned his head, "Well, your great-grandma must be pretty young; this building is just a little over fifty years old and has been closed for the past ten."

He continued, "Looking over the floor, I see no footprints or any indication that anyone has been here in quite some time. Treat this like a new case. I know the case is cold, but I'm guessing there is something more here than meets the eye."

The team approached the body with care; photos were taken from every angle before they got up close and personal with the body.

Vaughn walked over to Cody as he handed the wallet to the detective. After glancing at it, he showed it to Cody.

"Holy Moly! It's Abraham 'the shiv' Babel. Of all people, he should have known to never bring a knife to a gunfight!" Cody exclaimed. "Hey Vaughn, what have you got, a sixth sense?"

Abraham had been an assassin for the Jewish mob for fifty years. He specialized in silent death. Using Knives and other sometimes unidentifiable weapons, his targets never heard him coming.

"He was still a crack shot," Vaughn said. "He didn't enjoy making a lot of noise."

Something didn't look right to Vaughn. He had questioned Abraham a few times when working in New York. This body didn't appear tall enough and despite the "mummified" effects from dehydration and weathering, it just didn't click.

"Ask doc to run DNA and anything else he can get. Somehow this just doesn't sit right."

Several hours later, the body was taken to the morgue for a detailed evaluation. Vaughn continued to check out the club. As he wandered throughout the building, he recalled various fond memories of his youth before leaving Las Vegas for New York. He also remembered other not-so-fond memories of fights, shootings, overdoses and other evils of the times. He returned to Vegas a year before the club closed. It had gone from a hot spot to a dive, filled with hookers and drugs. *Times and things change,* he thought.

He stepped onto the balcony and looked down at the dance floor. There appeared to be something under all the grime and dirt. Vaughn called CSI Cody and asked him to return to the club. He needed a few more photos, and a police-contracted cleaning crew would arrive and work their magic when the place was cleared.

Cody arrived ten minutes later. "The cleanup crew will be here in about an hour," Cody announced. "What do you need, Vaughn?"

"Look down and tell me what you see. It looks like someone may have left us a message, if we are smart enough not to destroy it."

Cody looked down, "Holy Crap. I think you're right. Let me use a few filters to see if I can get a clear picture. Later we can superimpose the combined digital images on the computer and print out some poster-size slides for examination."

Before the cleanup crew was allowed on the scene, additional pictures were taken. A few hours later, Vaughn, Cody and U. S. Marshal Jake Samuels reviewed the large prints and the various computer overlays from the scene.

"It looks like we found Babel," Vaughn sighed. "The old man hasn't been seen in over five years. But I don't think this is him."

Marshal Samuels studied the photographs. "Take a look at this, Earl," he said as he overlaid the large prints. The three men were happy the prints were in clear plastic slides. They experimented on both the computer and with 20 x 24 inch prints to look at details. The four overlays exposed the message, "This ain't me you're looking for!"

Samuels tilted his head; he looked confused as he stared at the other two men. "You don't think old Abraham did this kill, made it look like it was him, and then gave us the clue to tell us it was someone else, do you?"

"Who knows," said Samuels, "He always loved to taunt us, daring us to try and catch him"

"Hey, take a look at this," Cody whispered as he ran his fingers over what appeared to be grey strands in the blood. A second message could be distinguished. "Yes I killed him and so many others."

Who killed who? Wondered Cody. "When we get the DNA back in a couple hours we will have half our questions answered."

The three men sifted through all the evidence found at the old club. The pockets in the clothing were full of trivia, junk collected from here and there. There were numerous match books, pens, a nail file, tokens from various casinos and foreign and American change. There was nothing with a good print or an indication of who had killed the victim.

Marshal Samuels was looking over the material when a light came on in the back of his head. "Do you recognize anything special about all this stuff?" he asked. "All these places have closed down. I think we have our clues."

Cody walked into the room, "I have DNA results and you were right, it isn't Abraham, it's Jeremy Slocomb." Sifting through a file, Cody read off the deceased's rap sheet. "He was a hitter ... but never made it to the big time. Here we go ...," he said as he laid the folder on the table. "In 1985, Abe and Jeremy crossed paths. According to the report, Jeremy attempted to replace Abe. The old man was hurt pretty bad, but Jeremy failed and Abe disappeared. It's my bet that

Abe came out of hiding and did a bit of payback on our friend in the morgue."

Marshal Samuels did some computer work. "I think I found it. Abe was sent to kill a high level drug dealer from South America that was here for a 'conference' with American business associates in February, 1985. Good old Jeremy thought taking out Abe would put him on the high road. Unfortunately, he made two mistakes: the hit wasn't sanctioned and he didn't finish the job."

Thirty years is a long time to track a ghost, thought Vaughn. He set up a computer search to review any similar finds in the area. *There are a lot of old buildings and if Abraham is still working the western states, he just might leave a trail.*

The computer search turned up eight additional killings all found by accident in empty buildings. Each murder site was identified by something in Jeremy Slocomb's pockets. The most recent was a six-month old body found not far from the club. Vaughn asked Marshal Samuels if he wanted to tag along. Vaughn had decided to check out some of the surrounding buildings, empty and occupied. Souvenirs from their victim's pockets matched some of the buildings and it would get him out.

There were no new bodies found, but on their tenth stop, they decided that someone was living in an abandoned massage parlor. "I remember this place," said Vaughn. "Busted it about a dozen times over the years. It closed up in 2009. The area got too rough, economy was for shit and they just went under."

Examining the doors, Samuels made an observation. "Look at this," he pointed to the scuff marks in the dirt."

"This door is being opened and closed on a regular basis. Probably homeless camping out or addicts using this place as a party house," Vaughn said. "But still, it wouldn't hurt to check it out."

Vaughn called the station, gave their location and situation. He asked for a squad as back-up. It didn't require a direct dispatch to just have the first car touring the area to stop. Addicts or Abe, it didn't hurt to have the cavalry on standby.

They entered without making a sound. Thanks to the broken windows, the room was dimly lit. The entrance looked abandoned, but there were fresh shoe prints in the dust. All the same size and style. There was soft music coming from the building's rear.

The "therapy" rooms had no windows. They checked each room

as they made their way down the hall. Both men used their flashlights in the rooms, but turned them off before continuing down the hall.

They reached what would have been the office where money was counted, deals were made and the girls could take a break without being disturbed. It was from this room that the music played.

Vaughn opened the door. Although not brightly lit, there were lights in the room. An old man was sitting in a wheelchair, his back to the door.

Vaughn and Samuels entered without a sound. They approached the figure from each side. Vaughn was the first to step into the old man's line of sight. "Hello Abraham," he said, "It has been a long time."

Abraham Babel looked up at Vaughn. "Hello, Detective, so nice of you to visit." Looking to his right, he smiled at Samuels. "Boy, I must be dangerous for the two of you to track me down."

Vaughn called dispatch, requesting formal backup and a van to take their old nemesis to the station. Samuels looked up to see a young man walk into the room.

"Who the F….." He started to scream as he dropped the bag of groceries and reached for the gun in his belt.

Samuels was faster; dropping to his knees, his hand was at his gun. In one smooth motion, his hand was up and the weapon triple tapped.

"NO!" screamed Abraham. His face went from smiles to confusion and fear as the young man fell backward from the room.

Abraham looked at the marshal with hate filled eyes. "That was my son." His voice broke. Shocked, Abraham hung his head and sobbed openly for several minutes.

Vaughn called for an ambulance when the shots were fired. He went to the boy. He was breathing. "He's alive," yelled Vaughn. "I have an ambulance on its way."

Everyone arrived at once. Five squads arrived as backup. The transport van and ambulance pulled alongside one another. For what seemed an eternity, the turmoil of so many people in such a small space was more than the old man could handle. He sat straight as a board, his face set in stone; his eyes staring out somewhere in space.

Coming out of shock, he grasped Vaughn's wrist, pleading, "Please, take me to him. Let me be with my son."

Vaughn felt sorry for the old assassin and wheeled him over by the paramedics. They watched as the medics worked with speed and efficiency, stabilizing the young man. Looking up at Abraham, one of them asked if he was a relative. "Yes, I'm his father."

The paramedic smiled. "Whoever did this should spend more time on the pistol range. Nothing vital was hit and barring any unusual complications, I believe he will live. We are going to take him to the hospital." He looked at Vaughn, "City General, see you there."

Abe slumped in the chair, but straightened when Samuels appeared. "Those medics just saved your life, marshal. If my boy dies, so help me, I will cut you into a thousand pieces. I may be old, but I still have talents."

"You should have taught him to keep his mouth shut and draw his gun," Samuels replied. "We're taking you to police headquarters for questioning, then to my office for more questioning. I'm sure we will file enough charges to keep me safe far longer than you will live."

Vaughn studied Abraham, "I'll check on your son and keep you posted."

"Thanks Detective. You're a good man."

Looking up at his two adversaries, Abraham smiled, "It's cancer, you know. I'm not going to live long enough to have a trial, but I still have time to get my revenge if something happens to Isaac."

Glaring at Samuels, he continued, "You best make sure my son stays alive until I'm dead and buried, marshal. You won't see me coming, but you will be screaming my name at the end." To prove his point, the old man's hand flashed from his lap blanket and imbedded a scalpel into the marshal's ribs.

Smiling, the old man said, "I need to practice my trade, nothing vital injured. Barring any unusual complications, I believe you will live."

One of the paramedics was standing behind Samuels. He moved the marshal out of harm's way and checked the wound. "We'll take you in the ambulance with the kid. A few stitches and you'll be fine."

Vaughn shook his head. The old Abraham was just as good as he was forty years ago. "Time to go, Abraham. That's a new charge to add to your rap sheet."

The old man smiled as Vaughn wheeled him out to the van. It was going to be a long but interesting evening as they questioned "the Shiv."

Funhouse

He stood inside the closet. There were no doors; the bright light glared into his eyes. He shuffled into the large room, stretching his stiff muscles. He hadn't moved for months and his body cramped as he tried to walk across the room.

Stepping into the light, he stared into the ice blue eyes and luscious lips of the female mannequin dressed as a ghoulish butcher with a cleaver raised above her head, ready to plunge it into the body of another bloody mannequin on the butcher block. It was then that he remembered.

Jack was always afraid of the dark. At thirty-five, he still slept with a light on in his room and a flashlight under his pillow, just in case. He seldom went out after dark because *"THEY ONLY COME OUT AT NIGHT."* He always carried an LED flashlight for unlit rooms, dark hallways and alleys for protection.

It was almost dark. Thanks to a meeting, he was late heading home and the bus was not on schedule. He began to worry. Darkness was approaching. He still had the ride to within a block of his home and walk from the bus stop on a street that had no lights. There would be no one sitting on porches or puttering in the yards this time of year; the overhanging trees blocked the light from the two streetlights on his block. It would be as dark as the inside of a cave and he would be forced to walk; no, he would run to the safety of his apartment building.

After ten minutes of standing in the last fading light, the bus arrived. The only empty seat was on the next to last row. Jack didn't like to sit in the back because "they" could be waiting there for him. He could be killed and the bus driver would not notice until he returned to the terminal. It had been a long day. Jack decided to take a chance and sit in the back rather than stand in the front of the bus.

The girl sitting next to the window was stunning, even by Jack's paranoid standards; she seemed as innocent as a newborn child. He saw no evil intent or a plan to use this girl against him by the various dark forces that haunted his waking moments. This specific seat appeared safe, even if it had to be shared with the woman.

She smiled as he sat down on the far edge of the seat. She scooted closer to the window, giving him a bit more room. She didn't notice her skirt creeping up her leg an inch or two, like small fingers groping for her waist.

The constant rhythm of the bus traveling the longer distances between the small towns calmed Jack. He dozed, floating somewhere between being awake and asleep. Fortunately, he didn't jump out of the seat and run screaming towards the front of the bus when the girl asked, "How far are you going?"

Coughing to hide his surprise, Jacked looked at the girl and mumbled, "To the end of the line."

"Great. This is my first time on this bus. Could you let me know the stop before yours?" She said as she held out her hand. "Kathy, Kathy Jackson. I just moved here from Chicago. I was transferred here. A promotion actually. I'm the new office manager for Monroe Insurance. I'm hoping I can make my mark here and move back to the city. It doesn't look like there is much to do around here," she rattled on.

"Um, Jack – ah Kinglsey," he said, looking into her deep emerald green eyes. He thought the color changed as he watched. He noticed glimpses of other worlds, other times, of darkness and light. Then, as if willed by an outside force, his eyes scanned the rest of her body, soft, full, complete, and suddenly, he wanted her. He realized he had never had this strong of a desire for someone since Sheila Burley in college.

Jack believed the way Sheila had humiliated him; had destroyed any physical desires he might have for another person. She had taken him to "lovers lookout," had him in the back seat, naked. She jumped out of the car as the football team started banging on the windows and laughing at him. Sheila made him get out of the car, naked. Laughing, with the team pointing and making fun of him, she threw him his underwear and they drove off. He walked home during the dark of the moon.

Word spread like wildfire that Jack had nothing to offer a woman. Jack accepted the rumors as truth and never bothered to develop any type of relationship with a woman.

Embarrassed by his leering, Jack looked into her eyes again and spoke softly, but with more confidence, "I've been riding this bus for twelve years. I work at Allied Computer Services as a programmer for the L-63-10. It's a computer that controls automated city functions. Except for human error in field situations, like the bus driver running ten minutes late tonight, I keep everything running on time. It wasn't because of the signals being out of sync synced or any accident that is running us late. Nope, just human error; everything runs on time because of me and the 63-10."

Jack forgot about the darkness and enjoyed the ride as he and Kathy small-talked as the ninety minute trip melted away. Sadly, Jack had just told her that she would be getting off the bus in two stops. As she stood to exit the bus, she saw the carnival.

Kathy squealed with excitement. "Look! They set up a carnival while we were working. Look at the lights and rides. Come on, let's go exploring."

She pushed him out of the seat, took his hand and pulled him to toward the front door of the bus. His fears forgotten, he followed her through the rows of colorful tents and sounds. They explored every show, rode every ride. Jack tasted foods he never knew existed. As the evening wore on, his smile grew. With growing confidence, he put his arm around her waist as they walked. He snuggled close and smelled her hair and perfume on several rides. She even laid her head on his shoulder as they began the "couples only" ride, filled with soft music and low lights. The cavern was filled with sounds of other couples finding more to do than hold hands during the ride. Jack, having a flashback of what happened in college, remained a gentleman.

It was almost midnight; the carnival was beginning to wind down. Even though it was a Friday night, outings didn't last long after midnight in this part of the country. People farmed or worked in the city. Staying up all night was saved for vacations away from home.

Kathy and Jack ambled towards the entrance. The games and shows had closed down. Rides were shutting down as the last of the passengers exited their seats.

Suddenly, Jack's fears returned as the field grew darker. He looked at his watch and realized he had missed the last bus. He stopped and fought for control of himself. His mind screamed at the thought of walking the mile home.

Kathy seemed to sense his anxiety and squeezed his hand.

Standing on her toes, she kissed his cheek.

His weak smile froze in place as he reached into his pocket and discovered he had lost his pen light. He was near panic when she stepped in front of him, smiling.

"I have a wonderful idea. Let's take one last ride. You can stay at my apartment tonight. I have plenty of room. You can catch the bus in the morning." Her smile filled Jack with promises he knew would never be fulfilled.

She grabbed him by the hand and began pulling him toward the last open ride. He stumbled when he saw the sign, "Fun House." It wasn't fun to him; it was a "House of Horrors." Kathy was taking him into the jaws of darkness; the place where his greatest fears lived, with the intention of devouring him, mind, body and soul.

Despite his fear, Jack couldn't say no to Kathy ... his Kathy. She would be his shining light and together they would finish the ride and go to her apartment. She would make up for all the evil Sheila had done to him so many years ago.

The attendant looked like a weasel with his thin face, long nose and growled something about hurrying along when he took Jack's money. "It's closing time."

Jack stifled a scream as they walked through the black curtains into a chamber as dark as hell. He didn't have the protection of a car; he had to walk directly into the face of evil. A black-light reflected its eerie blue glow on what may have been a door at the far end of the room. Kathy trembled with excitement as they walked, hand in hand, through the darkness.

They both jumped; Jack stifled a scream as they stepped on a creaking floorboard.

This little event was the first of many terrors introduced to Jack as they wandered the winding hall of blackness. There were spiders, werewolves, the mummy and more reaching out for him. Other terrors, too horrible for Jack to comprehend would spring to life and fill him with mind-paralyzing fear, bringing him to the edge of madness. The inset turned bright red and Dracula's coffin lid slowly raised as the master of the undead sat up.

Kathy, on the other hand, was having the time of her life. She would squeal with joy and excitement with each display of horror as she continued to drag Jack deeper into his fears.

Jack saw light at the end of the hall. His sigh of relief was silent, but powerful. He had survived and would follow Kathy to her home and reap the rewards of his bravery.

Instead, they entered a large, dimly lit room. They cast no shadows; Jack could make out shapes of furniture and other things that seemed to move through a mist surrounding him.

He felt tears running down his cheek. His fears had surfaced, but did not defeat him. He had stood his ground and felt pride that he continued to protect his woman through this adventure.

Kathy turned to him and put her arms around his neck. She laid her head on his shoulder and again softly kissed him on the cheek. Reaching down with her hand, she turned his head to hers and kissed him on the lips. Her tongue found its way into his mouth as she tightened her grip on him.

Ending the kiss, Jack moaned as she whispered once again into his ear. "You are very brave, Jack Kingsley. You fought all your greatest fears for me. I know this because I sought you out. You have won and will now receive your reward," she said as she stepped away and spread her arms wide as she turned in a full circle before him.

She faced him and she caressed his cheeks. "I invited you into my home, and here you shall stay. Not just tonight, but forever." She smiled as she continued, "You see, this is my home. I own the carnival. I travel around the world, seeing everything, doing anything I desire. I have no fear because my special friends at the funhouse protect me."

She kissed him again, "Once a year, I search for someone special. Someone who will join my family, serve as a protector, lover, friend, anything I need. Those who fail become food for my living displays. You stayed beside me, overcame your greatest fears, found in my funhouse, and tonight is that special night."

She reached up and kissed him again. This time it felt different. It felt as though he were being drained of all energy and spirit. Jack opened his eyes and looked over her shoulder. The shadows became clear as the mist lifted. Dracula, Frankenstein's monster, the ride attendant and all the creatures he had seen during the tour circled him as he felt his soul being sucked from his body to feed this beautiful creature.

Jack stepped around the ghoulish butcher and her plastic victim and shuffled his way toward the main room. Tonight was Kathy's special night. He had felt them enter the funhouse and make their way through the winding labyrinth. Unfortunately, not everyone can overcome their fears or desires. Her date had tried to run from his fears. Jack smiled. It was dinner time.

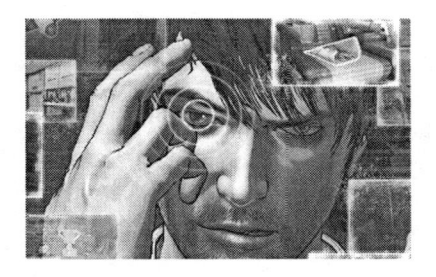

Tooth Fairy

I heard an unusual noise and crept downstairs to see what was going on. My guess was that my two dogs were playing a little tag and chase and had bumped into a coffee table or a wall.

Much to my surprise, I found a young girl coming around the corner to the stairs. She looked about twelve with long blonde hair and dressed in sheer white material. She looked like an angel, plus she had the wings to fill the part.

"May I help you?" I asked as she stumbled once again and fell into my arms.

"Oh … I … I'm looking for Timothy Jackson," she stuttered. "I'm the tooth fairy and I understand that he lives here."

I smiled, "Sorry, wrong house, he lives next door, but I'm afraid no one is home; they left on vacation this morning."

"Figures," she whimpered, "I've had a string of bad luck, behind in my quota and will be demoted to a polisher."

I offered my sympathies and asked her how many teeth she needed to collect to meet her quota. "Oh, I need around twenty-five to break even and thirty-two to finish out the month."

"Why don't you go to a dental office and collect the teeth that have been pulled? Don't they just throw them away?" I asked.

"No, they don't throw them away anymore, they crush them. I am at a loss and I try so hard." She began to cry.

"You know, you might want to consider going downtown. There are lots of homeless; their teeth can't be all that good, but most people should have a tooth or two that would meet your need. Offer them tooth money and take theirs. I doubt if you can be penalized just because of someone's poor mouth care."

"Hmm, the going rate is a dollar now. I'm sure there are some loose teeth on the street that wouldn't be hard to acquire. I would have to get several volunteers so there is a variety. But that just might work. I could even collect extras from the same person for next quarter." She smiled.

Suddenly, she spun a full circle, swinging her bag with both hands. It hit me square in the jaw. I felt my teeth rattle and a few floating in my mouth. I went to my knees. She looked me straight in the eye and said in a serious tone, "Better yet, I can start with you. Save some for another day ... do you live alone?"

With that, she hit me on the other side of my jaw. When I awoke, my jaw was broken; I had no teeth and a total of thirty-two "polished" gold presidential dollars in my hand.

Living Doll

~

    Simon was enjoying his Saturday afternoon foray of downtown boutique shops, eclectic bookstores and attic-find specialty stores. He wasn't shopping for anything in particular, but he had discovered and purchased a variety of unusual and old first edition books. Also among his bag of goodies were two fine historical photographs of rebel soldiers taken during the Civil War. Perhaps the best find of the day was an old cast-original replica of a black Model T Ford that dated back to 1908.

    Thinking about heading home, he decided on a whim to walk west one more block. The sun was low in the sky as he passed an antique store hidden at the end of an alley. The "World of Unusual Antiques" was a clapboard-front store with two bay windows burdened with clutter on either side of a dark blue wooden front door. In the old mullioned window to Simon's left was the object de 'art that had caught his eye from the street -- an ancient doll. Her hair was long, dark, and still as full as when she was new. Her ruby lips, pursed slightly, were welcoming and friendly.

    Curious, Simon entered the store and walked around a bit before getting a closer look at the doll in the window. Twice, the sales clerk asked him if he needed help. He played it cool, lowering the clerk's expectation of an impending sale.

    When he reached the window where the doll was propped against an old table, he gave her a closer inspection. The eager-to-make-a-sale sales person asked, "Would you like a closer look, sir?" Simon studied the clerk, a plain girl of twenty-something wearing a yellowed nametag pinned to an old cable knit, salvage-store sweater, read "Melanie."

    "Yes. That would be great, thank you." Taking the doll from Melanie, he strode to the worn wooden counter and laid the plastic-wrapped figure gently on the smooth surface. The plastic was yellowed and brittle. The doll was old but in remarkable condition. Either she had been well-cared for or she had been ignored or wrapped and stored in a covered box for many years. Her deep green satiny frock reminded him of his days at university back home in Germany. He found no obvious signs that she had been refurbished, which made her more valuable. Although the fabric of her dress looked new, the material that made up her body and limbs were brown with age, yet not falling apart. Her head and face were ceramic.

"She's a pretty thing," the sales girl said. "We've had her for over a year. She arrived as part of an estate sale. People look, but no one takes her home."

Simon saw a date on the back of her ceramic head which read "1773." As he unwrapped the doll, Simon thought of his eight-year-old daughter. She loved dolls and took good care of them. "Just out of curiosity," he asked, "how much would it cost to give this doll a home?"

"Let me check." Melanie picked up the doll and took her to the checkout counter where she opened an oversized, leather-bound book. She checked the table of contents then turned to a page with a photo and description of the doll. As she turned the book around for Simon to review she said, "All things considered, not a bad price, only $150.00."

Perhaps the price is what kept the precious thing in the window, he thought as he read the description. The doll, named Mary Philips, had been commissioned in 1772 for the daughter of a colonial officer.

In 1776, after the doll was delivered to the officer and his daughter, there were complaints that the doll disturbed everyone who came in contact with it. Many felt it was cursed. The family placed it in a box for storage sometime in 1778.

Although buried somewhere in the attic, both the major and his daughter continued to express concerns that the doll was trying to control their lives. Within two years, both the father and daughter disappeared. The doll was given to various family members over several decades. In the early 1920's, it wound up in an antique store.

According to the inventory sheet, the doll had moved from place to place, several owners had purchased and then returned it over the years; it had been found, abandoned in an attic and rescued as part of an estate sale in a small New England town just outside

Salem, Massachusetts in 2005. Since then, it had been in the hands of several antique stores until ending its journey at the "World of Unusual Antiques."

Interesting, Simon thought. *Illsa can add this to her collection.* Simon agreed to the price, wrote the check and headed home.

That night, he gave the doll to his daughter. She was delighted as Simon shared the history of the doll, its value, and the rarity of such a possession. Illsa said she would care for it as though it were her little sister.

The next morning, Simon discovered that Illsa had placed the doll on a shelf with her most prized possessions. He smiled to himself. He knew that she would talk to the doll and have it attend various tea parties sponsored by young Illsa. She would become a member of her growing list of make-believe friends.

A few weeks later, Illsa entered her father's office. "Daddy, I need to talk to you about Mary," she said weakly. She looked pale and shivered even though the home was quite warm.

"Of course, climb on my lap and let us have a talk." He wondered why she appeared so upset with a doll. This had never happened before.

"Daddy," she began, "Mary talks to me. She told me her name is not Mary but Elizabeth and that I should call her that from now on -- without fail." Illsa's voice was serious and tinged with fear and anxiety.

Simon studied his daughter, noting the pale color of her cheeks and the small dark circles under her eyes. He knew that she held conversations with her dolls all the time, and responded to what he assumed were their questions and comments.

Looking into her father's eyes, she continued, "Father, I don't mean play-talk like I do with my other toys. Elizabeth is talking to me. Just like you and I are talking now. At first, I thought she had a machine in her like my Talking Elmo but I can't find or feel anything."

Simon took a close look at his daughter. She was serious and believed all this was true. "Well, honey, what does Elizabeth have to say?"

"She told me that she is the spirit of someone known as Elizabeth Bathory. She said that the witch that made the doll called her spirit from the dead. The witch supported the English king." Illsa leaned close to her father and hugged him. "She says that she will continue her fight until America is destroyed or the English return to claim our country."

Simon was at a loss for words. He held his daughter in his arms and rocked her gently for several minutes. "Honey, no need to worry, Elizabeth can do nothing to hurt you. That war ended over two hundred years ago. I think we're safe."

"I told her that, but she won't listen Daddy … she frightens me. I'm not worried about me … I'm … worried about you," she whispered. "Elizabeth said she feeds off the energy of adults and frightened children. She told me that if you don't help in her cause, she will 'turn you into a pile of dust by the time she is finished.' She told me that once you are gone, she will enter me and turn me into an Angel of Vengeance." Looking into her father's eyes, Illsa continued, "She said if she can't return us to the English King, that she will join with an enemy to defeat America. Father, I believe that Mary … I mean … Elizabeth … is evil."

Simon considered all his options. "Tell you what. I will put Elizabeth on your top shelf and we will leave her there. Tell her not to talk to you. If she doesn't stay quiet, we will treat her like the witch she is and burn her in the fire pit."

With Elizabeth on the top shelf, life appeared to return to normal. When asked, Illsa said that Elizabeth was behaving herself. She would mumble ever so quiet and it didn't disturb the other dolls. Simon was happy because the problem seemed to be solved. He didn't want to destroy the antique doll, but he would if it brought peace to his daughter.

Weeks later, late one Friday night, Illsa was sound asleep and Simon was sitting in his favorite chair reading. He heard quiet footsteps coming down the hall. He assumed that his daughter was awake and coming to join him.

As the small footfalls stopped in front of the door, Simon looked up and was stunned. Standing as tall as her three feet would muster stood the doll -- Elizabeth. Simon wondered how Illsa had gotten her down from the shelf and placed her at the door. If Illsa thought this was funny, it was not. He would have a talk with his daughter once she appeared.

The doll was looking up at him. Simon dismissed the evil intelligence behind her eyes. "So…you are the master of this house?" It was a statement made with noticeable sarcasm.

Simon continued to stare, dumbfounded, at the revelation that he was being questioned by a doll -- an insolent one at that. He didn't respond. The joke wasn't funny, but he had to see what Illsa had planned. After all, it was Halloween. Putting down his paper, Simon found his voice. "Yes, I am. You should return yourself to the top shelf in my daughter's bedroom."

To his amazement, the doll walked across the room and stood in front of him. "Why don't you pick me up and put me on your lap like you do your daughter. It would be more comfortable and we can look each other in the eyes."

Simon bent over, cautiously picked up the animated doll and stood it on his legs. This thing inexplicably grinned, although a grimace was a better description. There was no mistaking that look in its eyes now ... evil.

"You know who I am, correct?" it asked.

"I know what Illsa told me. She also told me your story and I'm afraid that you are risking a nice home for a return to the antique store ... or worse if you continue to make threats against me, my daughter or this house."

The doll crossed her arms. "I guess you are not going to assist me in returning this country to the rightful king?"

Simon didn't know why he was talking to the doll.

"Well, first this country doesn't have a king; we elect a president every four years. Second, it has been over 200 years since the king of England lost the war and America gained independence. Today England and America are allies against tyranny. Therefore, the answer is no."

"You give me no alternative. If you are not with me, you are food." The doll lunged and bit into Simon's neck. She sucked his neck hard and deep. He felt his blood and energy draining from his body. *This can't be happening ... this can't be happening.* Shocked, he pulled her away, forcing her to release her heinous mouth from his neck. He held her out at arm's length.

"My, oh my ...," Elizabeth laughed, "You don't smoke, don't drink but chew a lot of gum ...you are bubalicious." She squirmed, attempting to reattach herself to his neck.

Simon stood and walked to the fireplace. Kicking the wire door open with the toe of his boot, he threw the doll into the fire. Simon heard the howls and watched as the doll stood on the burning logs.

"You aren't rid of me yet. You are too tasty to give up. I shall consume you and rule your daughter ... I will make her mine." Simon watched with relief as the green dress Elizabeth wore burst into red flames, licking up the fabric to her hair, and then her face. After a few moments, the doll turned to ashes. The all-consuming flame had eaten even the ceramic head.

Simon jolted awake. He felt his neck. It was tender, but there was no open wound. His rational mind overwhelmed, he stood, dazed and confused.

Filled with sudden fear and anguish, he rushed to his daughter's room, fearing the doll had killed his wonderful daughter. To his relief, she slept soundly; Elizabeth sat on the top shelf in her designated space. Realizing that it was truly a dream, he relaxed. Looking up, he saw Elizabeth turn her head and stare into his eyes. She smiled and blew a large pink bubble.

Showing her sharp teeth, she whispered, "Another time."

You Want It ... You Got It

~

"Okay, Dr. Jacobs, I've completed all the forms and signed the releases; I'm ready to discuss the experiment. I doubt I'll turn it down, I need the money," Steve said.

"Good...Good, my boy, but let me say that there is no payment for your work on the project. Your reward will be whatever you achieve in the next sixty days." Dr. Jacobs said with a distracted smile.

"I'm sorry doctor; I need the money for school, housing and just to eat," Steve said as he rose from the chair, ready to leave.

"Steve, just hear me out. You are the brightest candidate that applied for this project, and I'm not saying you won't make any money. I'm saying that it won't come out of the school research budget."

Steve sat back in the chair. He was curious as to the purpose of the experiment and how, without being paid, he'd make money, but at least the lecture included a free lunch. "Alright doctor, let's hear about this experiment and I want you to explain to me just how it is going to help me out of my financial troubles."

Dr. Jacobs explained, "The experiment is simple. I have developed a serum that allows lab animals to achieve their greatest desires. The last series of experiments had been done with apes that had excelled in raising intelligence. I witnessed them communicate with each other, work as a team and begin communicating with people using simple verbal language. After two years, they earned the right to live in an animal sanctuary without fences.

It's time to move up to some human experiments and experiences," Jacobs explained. "Unfortunately, the university believes that more studies need to be accomplished and verified before I use a human. The drug is safe and I need someone who can communicate their true feelings, goals, needs, wants, desires and how the drug helped them achieve their greatest dreams. In order to understand how the drug works, I need someone who can tell me what they do, what they accomplished and why they chose a particular action.

"Now, as I said, you won't get paid by the university, but let's say you invest a bit of money in the stock market. Your mind will grasp the complex issues of today's financial investment and you'll get rich in a few days. If you seek romance, you will automatically know what it takes to impress and perhaps seduce any woman anywhere. Whatever your desires, this serum will provide you with the mental and physical ability to succeed. With proper motivation, you may even be able to influence small groups of people, at least to a limited degree." Doctor Jacobs was literally bouncing in his chair from excitement. "However, there are a few requirements. First, you must keep an electronic journal with detailed information as to what you wanted and how you achieved it. I will review the journal from time to time so put all your thoughts and secrets in it. I'm looking for scientific information, not how you killed your roommate to get passing grades this semester, unless the plan was developed and executed because of the serum. The plan, not the act itself, will be most important when you write your reports.

"There is nothing you can do or describe that will shock me, and I will not inform the authorities of any of your actions. Second, you must return to the lab at the end of sixty days for a complete debriefing of your experiences and discuss anything you may have left out of your journal. In return, provided you are honest and detailed about your actions and achievements, I will provide you with a booster dose which will remain in your system for a full year."

Steve considered what the doctor had to say. He wasn't Mr. Popularity with his fellow students; even his roommate seldom talked to him. His grades were marginal and he was broke. If this stuff worked, he would be rich, popular and have an easy way to improve his grade point average. "What if I have more than one desire…can I achieve it all?"

"Yes, more or less, but you should take the day before your injection and decide what you want to accomplish, work it into a single statement and make it your goal. If you can combine several desires in that statement as subtexts, with practice, you can achieve anything. Let's say you want money; with money comes popularity, possessions and power. Don't just say I want to be rich…be specific, tell yourself what you want in the next sixty days and your mind will take you there. Your mind can also change your body and abilities; think outside the box. You can have more than one goal at a time, but I would start slow. You have plenty of time."

"OK...I'm in, but I don't want to start tomorrow. I want to think about my greatest desire and plan my goals. This is a lot to take in all at once," Steve decided. "I want to write a statement that will incorporate every aspect of my life."

"Not a problem, my boy. Tell you what. A week from today is the first of the month. Let's plan on starting the experiment then. It will be easy to track the two months and when you need to return."

The following week, Steve arrived at Dr. Jacob's office as agreed at noon. Dr. Jacobs reviewed the procedure over a cafeteria lunch delivered to his office. Steve signed another series of releases and a statement agreeing to tell no one about the experiment or its purpose. Steve agreed to go about his life, reach his goals and return in two months.

The IV infusion took a little over an hour. Steve read his goals several times out loud during the infusion and explained to Dr. Jacobs how this experiment would permanently change his life, all for the better.

As Steve was leaving the lab, Dr. Jacobs said, "Remember Steve, whatever you acquire is yours; however, you will pay taxes on recordable income and be responsible for other legal responsibilities associated with your actions, should you get caught doing anything illegal."

As Steve left campus, his confidence grew; he felt in charge of his life and possibly others. He saw fellow students and staff in a new light. He was now their equal, and in many instances, better than them. He had to prove it.

As a part of his desire, Steve wrote that he wanted to be a leader; he wanted people to obey his voice commands. He wanted people to fight over the right to complete a task that he suggested.

Heading toward the parking lot, he crossed paths with Lance Baker. Rich, popular, the quarterback on the football team and an all-state wrestler, Lance never acknowledged that Steve existed, even when they were lab partners last semester. Steve decided it was time to try out his new abilities.

"Lance...Hey Lance...Hold up buddy." Steve yelled across the parking lot. He ran and caught up with Lance. "Where you headed?"

Lance gave him a blank look. "Eh…I'm headed to my girlfriend's house. Ah, just who are you?"

Steve gave him a hurt look. "Lance, it's Steve, your lab partner last year; without me, you would have failed biology."

Lance's face smiled in recognition. "Oh yeah, I remember you now. Guess I tried to forget all that plant and animal stuff as soon as the final was over. Thanks again."

Steve liked the response and decided to push a little further. "I was thinking about heading to the offsite race track at the fairground; how about a ride?"

"It's out of my way, but why not. Mary Ann isn't going anywhere and she'll be happy that I'm just coming to pay attention to her."

Steve asked Lance to join him. The track was crowded, which added to his excitement. After looking at the odds and scanning a form sheet found on the floor, Steve had Lance buy tickets to several races. Steve was smart enough to let Lance pay for the bets; he kept them small, just in case he did win. He wanted to keep the winnings small. No need hitting a big pot full of money and drawing attention to himself.

In a couple of hours, Steve had won over $15,000 dollars. He considered this a good start and a way to open a checking and savings account in one of the national banks. Later, he would rent a safety deposit box and invest in the market. As they headed back to town, Steve said, "Why don't you take me with you. I've never met Mary Ann."

Lance shrugged as they headed back to town. Mary Ann was not happy with Lance for being late and bringing a friend. But Steve calmed the situation by explaining that it was his fault. Lance had talked so much about her; Steve just wanted to meet her and would appreciate it if Mary Ann would forgive the two them. Naturally, she complied.

Mary Ann was the head cheerleader and looked the part. Steve managed to convince Lance to sit on the couch and focus on the sports channel. Next, he convinced Mary Ann to perform a few special cheers just for him. Had there been music, it would have been called an erotic adventure. Steve complimented her on her abilities and flexibility and made a few other suggestions for his pleasure and entertainment.

He suggested she dance topless for one song and then explained it would be enjoyable to watch her muscles move as she danced nude. Mary Ann did as Steve requested without hesitation. While she performed her feats of erotic pleasures for Steve, Lance sat staring at the television. Steve experienced some of Mary Ann's other talents. He commanded that she should get rid of Lance and become his personal cheerleader. After all, Steve suggested, Lance took her for granted and used her as his personal plaything. Mary Ann didn't hesitate to agree with the suggestion.

On the ride back to the dorm, he commanded Lance to dump Many Ann. After all, there were so many other beautiful girls on campus, and Lance should never be limited to just one girl. On command, Lance promised to pick him up first thing in the morning.

Steve reported that the medication took effect within minutes of leaving the lab. His report included every activity; however, he used vague language, as he detailed his afternoon activities with Mary Ann.

He chose to let the old man use his imagination when the doctor heard the voicemail. That evening, he wrote a very detailed report on the electronic tablet. *This should give the old boy a heart attack*, he thought. Overall, it had been a good day.

The days passed. Steve continued to acquire wealth and some new friends. He convinced the school to allow him to test out of the classes he had failed in the past. He spoke with instructors and his grades were adjusted to honor-student status.

He bought a new car. His second greatest pleasure in life was filling several safety deposit boxes with money. He enjoyed winning at the track; he kept his winnings in the hundreds with reach race so there were no questions as to how much he was taking home. His stock market investments were also paying off. Had he claimed all his income, he would have been listed as one of the top 1,000 richest people under the age of thirty in America. He loved the idea of secret wealth and had the investment people give him bits of inside information without realizing it.

He also learned to control greater numbers of people. He called radio stations and over the air, controlled people to do his bidding. He wrote a short-short book and sold it for a large profit. While being interviewed on a local television station, he told everyone watching they should buy the book. He ended up on a national show and did the same.

Steve was proud of himself. He had met his goals. He had money, power over people and a lifestyle that filled Hollywood movie stars with envy. He managed to acquire a following of women who did his bidding without question and men who handled everything from running errands to giving him their homes and families.

Each day, Steve left general messages on the doctor's voicemail and detailed accounts in his electronic journal. He became far more descriptive of his actions and his control over others, his growing wealth and how he was able to travel on private jets and perform acts that would shock authorities and send him to prison. In other words, Steve abused his power far beyond that expected of a young impressionable college student.

The two months ended far too soon for Steve; he had new adventures lined up. He wanted to do some outlandish acts in public and was just getting up his courage. He believed that if Dr. Jacobs didn't give him the booster, he had enough money hidden away to live the rest of his life in comfort and, if his friends left him with his loss of powers, he would buy new ones. Overall, he saw nothing but blue skies and rainbows in his future.

He realized that he would never be able to kill again. The good news was he would pay cash to evade any illegal problems. With money and power he would employ the right people to take care of anyone causing him problems. Even if he didn't get the booster, Steve looked forward to an exciting new life.

He entered Dr. Jacob's lab at noon. Again, a cafeteria lunch was waiting for him. Dr. Jacob's said that he was disappointed in the lack of detail in many voicemail reports, but after reading the journals, he was impressed with the variety of activities Steve had accomplished. Steve provided a far more detailed report about his actions than he had put in any of his reports. He told story after story of his adventures; the people he controlled, killed and abused along with the money acquired from various activities that was not reported and hidden in a variety of banks.

Finishing his report, Steve decided to take advantage of his final few hours of power and said, "Dr. Jacobs, I would like to have the booster as soon as possible."

The doctor looked up from Steve's file and smiled. "Not to worry my boy. You have performed far beyond expectations. Your activities, as I said, were out of the box. I will take care of you shortly. I am hoping you will consider politics or some other occupation to expand your skills in the upcoming months; together we can make changes to the world -- changes that will make life on this planet wonderful."

The doctor continued to question Steve about some of his activities. Based on his daily reports and his detailed descriptions provided that afternoon, the doctor realized that his experiment had withheld a lot of information. At 4 p.m., Dr. Jacobs leaned back in his chair and smiled. "My boy, you have done well. Let's get that booster in you. Of course, I expect continued weekly summaries and a visit from you in a year, unless you are tired of all the success and want to return to being an average person."

Steve knew he had the doctor in his control and smiled. "Not a problem. I think I will record them in greater detail so I can review and relive all that I do; after all, a year is a long time. I wouldn't want to forget anything."

Once again, Steve signed a variety of releases and a confidentiality statement. He relaxed in the recliner as the IV entered his arm. He seemed to float on a cloud. He felt different, but under the circumstances, he didn't care. It was nice to be at peace for a change. His mind began to slow; the racing thoughts he had experienced during the experiment gave way to blank thoughts as he sank deeper into the effects of the drug.

"Now, my boy, I want to let you know that I am immune to your powers of suggestion. After all, it is my formula and I control how it works. I am recording our conversation. I want to get all the information I need without having to repeat myself. I want you to tell me where all your money is hidden, your open accounts, cars, boats, houses, everything and everyone you have acquired and kept during your adventure. When you tell me of the men and women you have under your control, tell me what they do for and to you."

It took Steve over twelve hours to relate all the accounts, numbers, addresses and possessions acquired over the two months. He provided a list of several students, adults and children that he continued to control. Steve informed Dr. Jacobs who provided sex acts, bought drugs, murdered and helped him travel around the world on their private aircraft and boats. He told everything. When he finished, Dr. Jacobs removed the IV and patted Steve on the hand.

"I want you to know Steve; you were the perfect test subject.

You had the highest test scores and a serious indication that you are a sociopath. Had you remained an upright citizen, I wouldn't be acquiring all your wealth and power. I was counting on you to use the abilities available to take whatever you wanted. You see, I am on the third booster, the one that lasts for a decade. My powers are ten times greater than yours. I will take command of all you have and grow my private kingdom from there. Some of your slaves will also become subjects to several other projects I have been working on. Many will serve my private needs and others will return to a normal life. Thank you for your service."

"Follow me," the doctor commanded. Opening a door, Jacobs stated. "Take this broom and sweep the maze, you will find food and water at different stations. If you can find your way out, I have another experiment for you to complete. I will check on you from time to time while you travel the maze."

Glass-eyed, Steve took the broom and began to sweep down the hall of the maze. He had no thoughts of power and control. Riches were unimportant. His one desire was to find the food and water waiting for him and to follow the trail leading to the next great adventure, even if it took all year.

A Night on the Couch

I woke with a scream lodged in my throat. The woman on top of me had obviously enjoyed herself. Her satisfied smile told me everything I needed to know. What scared me witless was the fact that she was fading. What disturbed me was I was wide awake.

I'm not sure what happened. I told my agent I was more than willing to travel the state of Illinois and southern Missouri doing book signings, but somehow, he continued to move me farther west. I guess I shouldn't complain; I was hitting all the major book stores and several small independents that favored my type of writing…dark fiction, horror, detailed descriptions of murders during the act of sex.

Thanks to a per diem payment, my publisher was meeting most of my expenses; food, gas money, with enough left over for a cheap motel and a small amount in my bank account. To help me in my travels, he provided a weekly direct deposit of royalties from book sales into my checking account.

True, I wasn't getting rich, but I was living the dream. I was making money, seeing the country and thanks to various locals, taking notes on the color and texture of towns for future stories. It's amazing how many people love to hold up the darker side of their town in the hope of seeing it in a book.

I had traveled New Mexico for the past two weeks. My publisher gave me plenty of travel time between signings, and on occasion, more than one signing in the bigger cities. I had several memory cards filled with photos of ghost towns, killing sites, multiple murders and even a few haunted locations where the spirits of the long dead continued to play out the last minutes of their lives.

In addition to the photos, I had several journals filled with notes, ideas and a few outlines for stories including several stories on my digital recorder.

I found myself in Taos signing books in a little independent book store that featured everything from up-to-date releases to old, out of print books and first printing books. To make it interesting, I was placed in the horror section of the store with a table and an assistant to run my errands.

Much to my surprise, business had been steady since the store opened. The manager asked if I would stay beyond my contracted four hours since people were still coming into the store wanting an autographed copy of my current book, *Deadly Madame*. I had no problem remaining at the table as people bought my book. The store was running low and they contacted another store in town to acquire their copies.

The morning turned into afternoon, followed by evening. I didn't know where the store was getting the books, but they kept me supplied and people continued to come to the table. There was never a line, but three or four people stood nearby to get my autograph and, at times, a picture.

Closing time arrived and once again, the manager asked me if I would mind staying another hour or so; he had received a call about a group of people on their way from Santa Fe. Two tour buses were arriving in the next thirty minutes.

How could I pass on the opportunity to sell over a hundred copies of my book at one time? I agreed, but said I needed to get something to eat. The manager said it was no problem and sent the assistant to get burgers and fries. At least there were still places to eat in Taos after 10 p.m.

Shortly after eating, the bus arrived. Books had once again appeared behind the table and I began autographing and posing for pictures. I lost count of the number of people who bought my latest release, plus some of my previous books. I had counted three hundred sales since closing time and people were still lined up. One of the older adults said that the driver mentioned the book signing at a truck stop and other tour buses joined the caravan. She said that someone on her bus had made a call and another twenty people from a local mystery writers group joined the caravan in cars.

This was my best event. I was looking forward to the three day drive back to Illinois. My plan had been the road when I left the store. Much to my dismay, it was three in the morning. I asked the manager about a motel in the area. To my disappointment, he said that there was a regional basketball championship in Red River and there wasn't a room available for over a hundred miles.

Tired and stiff, I said, "Well, if I can find some coffee, I will just start my drive home and stop at the first place with a vacancy."

My assistant spoke up, "If you don't mind sleeping on a couch, you can stay at my place. It's in Cimarron; you can follow me."

For the first time, I paid attention and took a close look at my helper. She was a lovely young lady; slim, nice smile, long black hair. Body art was showing under the sleeves of her blouse. "I wouldn't want to put you out. Besides, you don't know me and I don't want you to have problems with your neighbors."

Her smile went from ear to ear. "Not to worry. I am known as the 'stray lady.' I'm always bringing home strays to crash for a day or two. When I tell them who spent the night, I will be the envy of the building."

I looked at the manager for some sort of support. He smiled and said, "It's true; she's always helping out someone. I think she's gotten to know you today, and she's a good kid. Just so you know, she's an early riser and if you aren't careful, she'll inform the apartment building that she is entertaining a famous author and the word will spread around the neighborhood. You could find yourself having a book signing with all her neighbors. You might be stuck in New Mexico another day."

In everyone's mind, it was settled. I finished packing up and the manager gave me a count of books sold. I realized I had autographed over two thousand books and had my picture taken about the same number of times during my eighteen hour stay. This had been a successful day. I asked him how he got so many extra books. The average store stocked fifty or so books on hand for a signing.

"Easy," he said, smiling. "Redwing Books and Treasures and I pooled our resources and split the profits on the first two hundred books. When I saw how things were going, I called my brother, the local book distributor and had a van load delivered early this afternoon. I have twelve books left and would appreciate it if you would sign them -- one to me; another to your assistant, Julie; Cheryl, our cashier and the rest with just your signature. I think they will sell in a day or two."

I signed the books and left with Julie to follow her to her apartment and get some sleep.

We arrived at the St. James Hotel in less than an hour. I carried my overnight bag into what was once a sprawling hotel.

"They converted this place to apartments several years ago. I moved in right away because the rates were cheap." She rambled as we walked up the stairs to the second floor.

I was surprised to find a pleasant room filled with a variety of books and magazines. The couch didn't look particularly uncomfortable and I dropped my bag on the floor. Julie showed me around the apartment: a bedroom, living room, kitchen and bath. I estimated it to be around seven hundred square feet.

"Shower if you would like; I will make us a quick snack. I always need a bit of time before I settle in for the night."

I took a quick shower, put on sweats and went into the kitchen. She was baking something that smelled heavenly. In less time than it takes to drink a cup of coffee, we were eating sweet rolls and Julie was telling me her life story. She left home at eighteen, dropped out of college and found the job at the bookstore where she had been working for the last five years. She was single, happy and enjoying her life. "I have read all the books shelved in the living room and recently, started adding shelves in the bedroom. Books are my old friends and I can't seem to abandon them to a library," she said.

Finished, she bid me good night and headed to her bedroom. "Oh, I almost forgot. We may have visitors; if you don't want to talk, just tell them. I sometimes sit and talk with them until dawn."

The look on my face must have shown my confusion. "Oh," she said, "I guess you didn't know the St. James is haunted. They get lonely sometimes, and being the 'stray' lady, they all come here. Don't worry, they're harmless. Good Night."

I stretched out on the couch and immediately fell asleep. Sometime before dawn, I felt someone join me on the couch; it shifted as someone straddled my feet. It was dark; I was bone tired and didn't bother to fully wake up. I thought it might be Julie trying to wake me and have a bit of fun with a middle-aged, out-of-shape horror writer.

I mumbled something and fell again into a deep sleep. I didn't realize my blanket had been removed or my pants pulled down. My next memory was of someone sitting on me, riding me with full abandon. I write these things but never experienced the effects of someone's lust.

I was forcing myself awake as the early morning light was beginning to come through the windows. I opened my eyes to see the outline of a woman in the final states of sexual abandon. Her scream was silent but her actions were earth-shattering.

I jumped, fully awake with a scream lodged in my throat. The woman on top of me had obviously enjoyed herself. Her satisfied smile told me everything I needed to know. What scared me witless was the fact that she was fading. It didn't help that I could see through her even though I was wide awake. I watched as she bent over. Her touch was light as a feather as she stroked my cheek and kissed me on the lips.

Julie stood across the room, watching with a large smile on her face. "Congratulations. Mary Lambert took a liking to you. In case you're wondering, she was the wife of Henry Lambert, one of the founders of this place. She died in 1926 and is one of my shy ghosts. Up until now, she would make her presence known to no one but me. You must have special powers to attract Mary. I'm sure this was an experience you have to write about soon. Let's start the morning with some coffee?"

I got up and showered once again. Shaken, I sat at Julie's kitchen table and we talked. We discussed the ghosts, my visitation and the possibility of what it all meant.

Around noon, I headed home. I told Julie I would like to return if she didn't mind company. She promised that there would be another book signing at the store when my next adventure appeared in print. As I was leaving, Julie smiled at me, "Who knows, I will ask Mary if she's willing to share you on your next visit."

I wonder why I am in such a rush to return to the bookstore. Was it Mary or Julie that interested me? While driving, I realized this last adventure was a source for more books than I would ever have time to write. If I could talk to ghosts, I could bring out secrets they would want told, and do a little exaggeration about their everyday lives.

If things go well, I just might see about moving into the St. James Hotel, that is, if the ghosts and the 'stray' lady will have me.

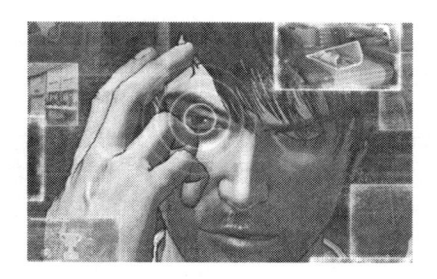

Dark Window

Gibson spent many of his evenings staring out the picture window facing the forest beyond his patio. He didn't care much for the great outdoors, so the patio was devoid of furnishings, except for a fire pit built into the deck and a chaise lounge the local wild life used to sun themselves on summer afternoons.

Gibson seldom turned on his living room lights at night. There was no need. He read in his bed, watched television in the living room and ate in the kitchen. As far as he was concerned, since he had no wife or children, the family room was destined to be his thinking room. He often sat in his recliner and stared out the window. His thoughts produced a variety of potential stories and adventures. He had always been a loner. His imagination was his best friend, and his computer converted his mental adventures into a series of short stories and novels. It allowed him to live twenty miles from his nearest neighbor. He preferred to deal with people by phone or email or, when forced, to meet them face to face when he went into the city for a conference or shopping.

Gibson often visualized his stories. He considered it a cheap way to go to the movies. He placed himself in the adventure to sit and watch the action. As far as he was concerned, this was a great life. He would stare out his window as the sun set and often rose from his chair as streaks of morning light began to cast a long shadow over his shoulder.

Gibson sat, eyes closed. He relaxed with a quart of iced tea beside him. He let his mind wander. He needed a couple of short stories and some ideas for a novel.

He squirmed in his chair, finding his comfort level, he sighed and opened his eyes. He was greeted by the site of a face with two large eyes staring back at him. Gibson froze. There wasn't another living soul within miles of the house. He decided it had to be some sort of reflection from the fire behind him. He closed his eyes and opened them again. The pair of eyes remained just above the windowsill.

Gibson sat as still as a statue; he continued to stare unblinking at the illusion standing on the other side of his window. Several seconds passed before he realized that someone was trespassing on his land. He would have none of that. Slowly, he rose from his chair. Stepping backwards, he reached the fireplace, raised an arm and removed his rifle from the rack.

He continued to stare at the eyes as he chambered a round and slowly walked to the sliding door beside his window. Gibson didn't smile or give any indication that he wanted to be friends. He wanted no human contact. He lived his life the way he wanted. If he allowed people to disturb him, they would change his lifestyle, forcing him to talk, cook proper meals, dress before noon and not be allowed to wander around his property when he wanted…day or night.

Gibson slid the door open and stepped out, his rifle pointed in the direction of the intruder. He froze. The two eyes were lifted by a pair of stalks coming out of an oblong head. The head was attached to a soft-looking body that resembled an odd shaped stress ball.

Turning, the creature faced Gibson head-on. The pair of eyes rose on their platform to look directly into his eyes. A soft whisper emitted from the creature, "I come in peace."

Lowering his rifle, Gibson entire body shook as he muttered, "I've never wigged out in the five years I've lived here." He turned and walked back into the house. The creature followed.

Gibson collapsed in his chair. He couldn't form a description of the creature; its shape changed when it moved across the room. Standing, or whatever it was doing, not five feet from him, the creature adjusted its height, so the two remained eye-to-eye.

"Okay, fella. You're the intruder. Tell me what's going on and why you are here." He had accepted the creature as real and decided to take a direct approach in finding out what it wanted, and then shoot it or get it the hell off his property.

It seemed to vibrate and Gibson heard the whispered voice, "My ship, it crashed in the woods. You are the only dwelling nearby. I need to make repairs and a place to survive until I can leave."

Gibson sat for several minutes. Finally, he shook his head. "You expect me to believe you are real and not my current fantasy adventure? You want me to help you until you can leave my property to return to space?"

"Yes," it whispered. "My needs are few. It would help if we could bring the ship to your dwelling. I can make the repairs myself, but with your help, all can be completed in a short time."

Gibson considered the proposition. If his mind was creating one of his fantasy adventures, it would make for interesting writing. If it was real, it still made for interesting writing, especially if he could get the creature to tell a few space tales.

"I understand your desire to get off this rock. But I have to ask, what's in all this for me?"

The creature considered the question. "I can help you improve your dwelling. I will remain out of your way; it is obvious you demand a great deal of privacy. I will assume a form that is pleasing to you. I am sure this form makes you uncomfortable."

Gibson added, "You must tell me about your adventures on this planet and others. I will retell your adventures as stories. All this is agreed upon, yes?"

"Yes," the creature agreed. "You must not allow anyone to know of my existence. Governments would lock me away. It has happened to my brothers in the past."

"Agreed," Gibson said, smiling, holding up the current copy of his favorite sports magazine. "Now as to your form…" The creature began to change shape. It grew in height, solidified and Gibson found himself staring at what he described as a naked Sports Illustrated swimsuit model.

"Will this meet your requirements?" it asked with a voice that could melt ice and harden steel. Gibson stared opened-mouthed at the beauty.

"You may call me Shirley," she said.

Gibson found a shirt that fit her like a mini dress. He could not keep his eyes off her as she received the tour of his house. "There are four bedrooms, three baths, a large kitchen, living room, this den and the deck. I have the master bedroom; you can choose your room and we should get along fine."

Shirley and Gibson returned to the den. She sat on the divan opposite the recliner. "My needs are simple. In my natural form, you would call me a semi-solid. I must return to my true self from time to time. I am what you would call a night person; your sun will destroy me. I consume liquids and semi-solids as nourishment. Since all is agreed, can we get my ship?"

Shirley returned to her gelatinous form and seemed to float in front of Gibson as they made their way to the tree line. The ship had landed in a clearing. It did not face his window. Gibson wondered how he hadn't heard the crash; until they reached the ship.

It resembled a squid; long, cigar shaped with appendages. The ship was not heavy and between the two of them, they maneuvered it to the patio within the hour.

Gibson examined the ship. "How do you plan to fix this thing? It looks more like a living creature than a form of transportation."

Returning to human form, Shirley ignored his question but said, "It can't stay out here during the day; like me, it will dry out. It must be protected."

Gibson considered the problem. "I have a two-car garage. I can move my car and we can put your ship inside, cover the windows and begin repairs."

Shirley examined the garage and agreed it was adequate. Once again, they moved the ship. Gibson covered the windows with plywood. The area was light tight. Both parties were satisfied with their work as the first light of dawn began filling the sky.

The two returned to Gibson's cabin. "Tomorrow we begin making repairs," Shirley commented. He continued to wonder how the ship was damaged and repairs could be made when the whole thing resembled a half-filled water balloon.

Shirley went upstairs and chose a room, entered the closet and returned to her normal state. Gibson said good night, retired to his room and considered the story possibilities. As he drifted off to sleep, he decided this hallucination was the start of an interesting novel.

Gibson was up and about around noon. Coffee in hand, he started his new story, "Blob from space." It flowed well and ended with the craft stored in the garage. He did not include Shirley's morphing abilities, at least not yet. He wasn't particularly comfortable with the feelings he experienced when Shirley was in human form; she may look human and desirable, but he knew she was not much more than a water balloon.

At dusk, he heard the guest shower running and realized she was up. He wondered why she showered; after all, as a semi-solid, couldn't she rinse herself off and be clean? He decided to ask if he had the opportunity.

Shirley entered the kitchen and appeared to be swelling at her seams. Smiling sheepishly, she explained that she not only required liquids to survive, but had to fill herself to the point of exploding so she could "feed" the ship. The water would convert to a semi-solid nutrient, allowing the ship to repair itself.

As darkness fell, the couple walked to the garage. Gibson unlocked and opened the doors; the ship floated out. He pushed it to the patio and secured it to the railing. Per Shirley's instructions, he managed to push his finger into the ship. Shirley walked up behind him and ran her arms around him. Holding his hands, she used his finger as a pick and inserted her hand into her vessel. He felt his fingers tingle as she transferred the water from her body into the craft, but thought nothing of it.

They stood for over an hour. Shirley remained in human form and told Gibson of her adventures on Earth. She had no shyness as she explained the various experiments she had performed with a variety of humans and other species.

"I enjoyed joining with dogs and other non-human life forms. It was quite the experience," she explained. She didn't explain what she meant by joining, but he let his imagination keep him from asking questions.

With the job complete, the ship began to radiate a pale pink luminance. "It will take more infusions to heal the ship," she explained. She wrapped her arms around his waist and kissed him on the back of the neck, thanking him for his kindness.

He shook his head in wonder. If she couldn't puncture the ship in her own form, how did she enter and travel within its confines? He decided it was another question to ask when the time was right.

Gibson's story had taken a life of its own. He incorporated the stories she told him at night, along with their "feeding" of her ship. He also increased the tension of the story by adding romance between the two of them. His fantasies concerning the graceful creature exploded on the page. He knew it could never happen, but it livened up the novel.

Within the week, he and Shirley were sitting on the patio. The ship was secured in the garage's confines. Both were sipping iced tea and staring at the stars. "You do realize that I will leave here tomorrow night," Shirley said.

"So soon?" his shocked voice whispered. For all his desires to be alone, he had somehow grown attached to the creature sitting across from him in a faded shirt, half buttoned.

"My ship is ready. I wanted one last night with you before I go." Her body shimmered in the moonlight. "It isn't easy, making a friend, a life saver, and then having to depart."

"Stay," Gibson said as he stood and walked over to her. He was prepared to beg. He would promise anything to entice her to remain with him. He had the thought of puncturing a hole in the ship so she would never leave him.

"I know you mean well, but you really wouldn't harm my ship. You are not that kind of man," she said sweetly.

"How…How…? You can read my mind?" he asked, confused.

"As problems developed with my ship, I sought a safe location. I read minds from all around. You were the individual I required. You can be trusted. You are honorable. I knew you would be willing to do anything to help a lady in distress, no matter the circumstances.

"You stayed, even though you knew the type of thoughts I had about you."

Shirley nodded her head and put her arms around him. They kissed, softly, tenderly. To Gibson, it felt like something between kissing a sister and his first kiss from his girlfriend at the age of ten.

Slowly, her response grew in passion. It felt like his prom kiss in high school. His hands unbuttoned the shirt. She stepped into him. Somehow, Gibson found himself lying on the deck, naked. She was on top, riding him like a banshee chasing townspeople.

He rose to kiss her. At that moment, she returned to her natural form. Semi-solids, Gibson, I require semi-solids. Water is wonderful, and it keeps me and the ship from becoming dust, but it is not nourishment. I require the vitamins, minerals and other things found in your blood, skin, bones and body." He heard her whisper, "Your finger provided just enough to keep my ship alive, but not enough to heal her."

She engulfed him like a giant amoeba. Gibson tried to scream, kick, and dig his way out. It was too late; he was trapped. His body faded into a cloudy liquid within her skin's confines. She heard his final thought, *so dark, just like looking out my window at night.*

She stood, stretched and began to float to her ship. Now fed, she was able to force her body through the outer hull. She shared the meal with her counterpart. Together, they floated from the garage and began to rise.

Shirley looked forward to returning to her home. Her people would be thrilled with her stories from earth. This planet would feed them for years.

Open All Night...
Donors Welcome

    Reporter Nick Myers sat in the doorway, sinking deeper into the shadows as the sun set. Across the street, the Hillside Blood Bank was closing for the day. The last employee passed through the exit as the door closed. He knew that in another hour the "Other" blood bank would open, welcoming anyone who passed through the doors: drug addicts, winos, hookers, anyone willing to roll up their sleeves.

    Nick had heard about "Open All Night...Donors Welcome" through his contacts on the street. The bank paid premium dollars to those willing to become "regular donors." A regular donor required extra names and gave blood more often than the required 56 day recovery period. His contacts explained that the names were kept in the computer, just in case the authorities investigated the bank's procedures. Every "night donor" was provided with a profile that allowed them to qualify no matter their habits or health.

    Intrigued, he decided to investigate the place before offering the blood bank as a possible story. After all, the *National Conspiracy Quarterly* thrived on tales of the unusual. Nick didn't want to pitch the story idea to his editor without verifying the facts. Distributing bad blood into the marketplace would close the only blood bank in the area, even if the day workers knew nothing about the activities going on at night. And on a personal note, he had a reputation to maintain.

    He spent his first day checking the building. No back door or windows; there was no special employee entrance. Except for the front windows and entrance, the place was a brooding fortress of stone. Everyone and everything had to come and go through the main door.

    There were more than hours of operation differences between the two businesses. South Town shipped their blood for processing right after the last completed donation. Everything was packed and taken to the local hospital for testing, processing and distribution to those in need. Staff, donors and supplies entered and exited through their front door.

"Open," on the other hand, operated in a quite different manner. During the day, donors came and went, vendors came and went and staff would occasionally leave the building. At night, the doors were left unlocked so donors could enter. Nick realized that the staff never entered at night or left before dawn. They simply appeared as soon as the sun went down. Nick started counting people; he realized on any given night, more donors would enter than leave.

Nick interviewed the neighboring business managers and staff about the blood bank. He received vague answers. They knew nothing about the other blood bank. The blood passed state inspections, their certificates were on the wall at reception. They said there was no special or adjoining basement entrance or exit for staff or supplies to come and go.

When he spoke to the blood bank manager, she said, "To be honest, it's of no concern to us what people think. Our evening operation is run through an outside source and serves a different clientele. The product goes to a privately contracted market and their operation does not concern us." She also informed Nick that Hillside Blood Bank was not open at night. "We don't know the name of the evening operation and frankly, it is none of our business and for that matter yours." she said walking away.

Nick was lost in thought, but focused on the blood bank when he noticed the nightly line forming at the front door. Donors, lost souls in search of something, stood impatiently. It reminded Nick of addicts standing outside a clinic, waiting for a fix. He realized the faces of the "early birds" had changed over the last couple weeks. This was a whole new group wanting to be first to provide their "gift of life" before continuing on their road to nowhere. Curious, Nick waited until there were several more people in line before he stood and walked up to one of the donors, hoping to strike up a conversation. He chose a spot away from the front window and out of sight should someone look out.

"Got a light?" Nick asked the woman. Her eyes reflected a hunger or perhaps a hurt that extended far beyond the booze, drugs or abuse she had experienced in the past. Her eyes darted from side to side and she stood straighter, fearing someone would grab her and take her away her place in line.

"No. And don't even think you can cut in front of me, either," she said in a low pitch that warned him.

Nick decided to try a new approach. "What's so special about this place? Why is everyone waiting for this blood bank to open? Going to make a withdrawal?" he said with a chuckle.

"No," she said, somewhat calmer, realizing that he didn't want to enter the bank. "The more we donate, the more we make. They fix it where we make blood faster and can donate more often. I can come every three days now."

Nick nodded and walked down the line, observing faces, body language and actions. He would stop every now and then. With each stop, he gathered more information. He began to put a picture together.

The sun had set when Nick reached the back of the line; he slid into place. Noticing the line begin to move forward at a decent pace, he decided that the bank was in full operation. He watched as everyone advanced and realized he had not seen any of the early donors leave.

He reached the plate glass windows at the front of the building. He considered walking on when he noticed certain people were handed one of three colored, printed cards and sent to the back. Others were required to sit in a booth for screening.

At the front door, Nick almost walked away. He considered his options and decided that the best way to discover the truth was to take a look inside. He knew that until they put the needle in his arm, he was free to change his mind about donating.

The receptionist was pretty enough, even though the fluorescent lights gave her a pasty green color. "You're new," she said unsmiling as she looked up at Nick. She began taking general information; the same questions asked at any blood bank.

He moved to a screening booth where the next person did not ask him the usual questions about health and safe living habits. Instead, the questions revolved around family, friends and social aspects. It would appear that they wanted people without friends, family or anyone who might miss them. The last question was, "Why do you want to donate, today?"

The question caught Nick by surprise. "Well," he paused, "I've been out of work for a while, and I heard that you have a special program that will allow me to make more money. If it keeps me in lunch and bus fare, I can get around town and look for work."

The screener smiled. Her pearly white teeth seemed to flash for just a second, giving Nick an odd feeling that something wasn't quite right with her mouth. *Dentures*, he thought.

"OK, I'll put you in our fast track program ... first door on the right as you go down the hall," she instructed.

The next morning, Nick thought about his blood donation. The bank was clean; everything was disposable -- just like any other blood bank. Except for the little "booster" shot he received after his donation, nothing appeared out of the ordinary. The nurse explained that the shot would help him produce more blood, and he could donate in four weeks.

Every evening, Nick found himself tucked away in the shadows, sometimes in a doorway, other times in an alley. Watching, waiting to figure out what was happening to the blood and many of the donors. One night, he kept an exact count of the comings and goings of customers. There were twenty-two people that checked in who didn't come out. All twenty-two were given the fast track cards.

Nick decided that the blood had to be finding its way to the black market. He smiled as he thought about the fame he would receive when this story broke. Fear of contaminated blood entering the general population would cause a panic, the blood bank would come under closer examination and the nightly activities on the poor helpless souls would end. Of course, to get his paper to even consider the story, he would have to discuss the possibilities of ghouls or vampires. He decided to hold off talking about the story until he knew the truth.

By the end of the second week, Nick had an itch. He couldn't put the feeling into exact words. He realized that he was hot all the time and he felt as though he needed something. *A Fix, they injected me with a time-released chemical that will make me an addict.*

It was almost dawn when he entered the blood bank near the end of his third week. The receptionist looked up. "Back so soon," she said. "You're not scheduled for another donation for another week."

Nick stared at her. He didn't know what to say. As he thought about the regulars, he knew their problem and pain as his "NEED" reflected in his expression. He breathed a sigh of relief when the receptionist said to hold on a minute, she would get a nurse.

A tall, dark-haired woman walked to the counter and looked at him; no, she looked through him as though she were counting the red blood cells in his body. "It looks like your body reacted well to our serum and is producing blood faster than the norm. You are more than qualified as a fast track candidate," she said. With a sharp nod of her head, the receptionist handed him a different colored card. She pointed to the screening booth where the raven-haired nurse gave him a shot and sent him on his way to the donor room.

As Nick glanced at the card, he realized that his name was now Mr. Frank Donor. He smiled as he was escorted back to a donation table. Once again, the procedures seemed appropriate, he was given a second shot before leaving the building.

Nick realized that the "itch" began sooner and with a greater intensity with each visit. He was now donating every three days. He was always given an injection before the donation and after. When he asked, he was told that the injection increased blood production, causing him to have the hot spells. According to the nurse, there was nothing to worry about.

He decided it was time to get the dirt on the operation, get his story written and return to a normal life before he became one of the missing donors. He decided to take a chance. Tonight, instead going through the regular first door on the right, he entered the door at the end of the hallway.

He found himself in another room filled with chairs used to take blood. He sat in one in the far corner. It provided him with a view of the entire room and down the hall, yet eliminated the possibility of someone sneaking up on him. He left the door open but was ignored by the staff and other donors as they continued their regular routine.

He had remained awake all night, dawn was approaching and he was ready to walk out when a nurse entered the room. Smiling, she checked his card, prepped his arm, inserted the needle and gave him the first booster. Nick blacked out.

Through the darkness, he heard a voice. As the world returned in shades of gray, he heard her say. "Mr. Donor, you were once again ahead of schedule, and entered the wrong room. Your failure to follow procedure by entering the private donation room made us a bit suspicious."

Nick focused his eyes on Nurse Selene and realized she held his wallet. If they had his wallet, they knew he wasn't one of the derelicts frequenting the bank. "This room is for the last stages of participation by our patrons. I see you are a writer and journalist. I hope you weren't trying to do a story about our little feeding ground."

His head felt fuzzy and his mouth filled with cotton. He attempted to answer, but couldn't get words out. Nick attempted to sit up and remove a needle in his arm. But he couldn't to move. The nurse was going through the remainder his billfold.

She knew. He was fastened to the table. She knew everything. "So," her voice filled with sarcasm, "is this an assignment by your editor or were you going to freelance, Mr. Meyers?"

His expression told her everything she needed to know.

"I see. You thought you could invade our sanctuary and create some sort of story. I hate to tell you, but you are not that well known and when you disappear, no one will miss you. No one knows or cares where you are or what you are doing. Who will miss you, Mr. Myers?" Again, the sarcasm ripped a hole in his heart.

"Granted, your blood is very strong and reproduces faster than our average…client. My guess is you are quite the healthy specimen; however, you weren't properly primed. We will provide you with boosters, your production will continue to increase by volumes, but will end far too soon. Such is life, so to speak." She sighed. "Your blood will cease production in a matter of weeks, but it will be oh so sweet, for someone, while it lasts."

Nick looked around the room and realized that six other chairs held donors. Now he knew why everyone entering the blood bank failed to come out of the building after their donation.

"Who knows, Morlock may like your creativity and decide to keep you among us? It has been many decades since someone new has joined our clan." She laughed. She gave him another injection in his left arm. The table began to sink into the floor.

She flashed a smile; Nick realized that her teeth were also too perfect, too white, the canines far too pointed.

His heart pumped like a racehorse in the home stretch. Fear, the ever-present thread he had in all his stories, went from an adjective to a proper noun. He turned his head. He didn't want to see the door closing above him. He was trapped on a table, in a cavern of indirect light. He sank far deeper than in an average basement.

He stopped moving. Looking around, he saw tables, rows of tables paired with the inclined chairs. To the left, the stationary platform held a body. To the right, he saw the donor chairs. Joining the two was a thin plastic tube transporting blood from the donor to the thing that slept and consumed life-giving blood.

"Mr. Donor, so good to see you again." He recognized the voice of the raven-haired woman.

He noticed his chair was on some sort of turntable. As he turned into position, a second chair was moved into place and prepared to rise back up to the donation room.

"Here we are. Welcome to your new home. Allow me to introduce you to Jonathan Morlock, Order of the Dragon, Knight of the Templar, Majesty of the Valgrade Empire from 1500 to 937 BC and Keeper of the knowledge of the black arts of Zanzibar."

The voice droned on as the woman wiped a husk of what appeared to be translucent paper from the chair his had replaced, just before it was positioned and began to ascend through the ceiling to await the next arrival. Nick realized that it was all that was left of a body after a complete draining.

"Poor Master Morlock can no longer hunt or even feed in the outside world. He is far too old, yet we don't want to lose his knowledge. So, you will care for him, these others and on occasion we treat ourselves by blood transfer. The IV will take your blood and give it to the Master." The voice laughed as she joined the tubes. "Not to worry, you arrived just in time, even though it was sooner than planned. I doubt you will last long. No offense, but no one survives more than a few weeks. Mr. Morlock is always very hungry."

Nick shifted and stared up into the darkness as he felt his heart continue to pump, feeding the thing that lay beside him.

Follow That Man

Jim Thornton drove the only taxi in Bryman. The California town was small; the four-way stop light in the middle of it was more of an income generator than for public safety. Most people walked around town, although many had cars for going to the city. Jim's Taxi served the older population who were unable to walk the eight blocks across town. He would take them to the general store, pharmacy, library and the town's only restaurant. During spring and early summer, he would take people to the square for the high school band's concerts.

Needless to say, Jim was surprised when a young girl, perhaps all of thirteen came bounding down the steps and climbed in the back of his cab. He turned to get a better look, then smiled and said, "Where can I take you, young lady?"

She studied him for a moment, trying to decide if he was being sarcastic, deciding the guy was doing his job. "You see that Mexican restaurant across the street?" she asked. "Well, in a few minutes, a man is going to come out of there, and I want you to follow him."

Jim was surprised at the request. "Young lady, I am not a private detective and my service provides people with transportation to places they can't get to on their own."

"Look mister, if he sees me, I'm dead meat. I've got to know what he is up to. You see, he's my stepdad; we all went on vacation last week, and when I woke up this morning, they were gone. I saw his car parked in front of the restaurant and peeked inside. He's alone. Alone, do you know what that means?"

Jim gave it a few seconds thought and shook his head no.

"It means he has done something to my mom, and I will be next. He will get the house and everything we own. I have to find out what he has done with her. I have to find her before he kills her. Look, here he comes."

Jim glanced over and saw a rather short, balding man getting into an upscale town car. "Okay, I'll see where he goes, but you are paying my regular rates and if I get another call, you are out on the side of the road."

"Here, take this as a deposit," she said, handing him $20. "That should buy me enough time to discover what he's done to my mom."

Jim took the money and calculated the girl was good for forty miles, provided they didn't have to stop and wait on the guy or didn't decide to waste time at the general store.

His cab was obvious and easy to see so Jim decided to travel along for a block or so, pull over, and then catch up with the guy. Never losing sight, but hoping the man didn't realize he was being followed.

Once they left the town limits, there was no fooling the man. He would recognize the yellow taxi and know he was being followed. The good news was that there was only one highway in and out of Bryman, so Jim hoped the other driver would assume the cab had someone going to a neighboring town.

A half mile past the city limits, the car turned off onto a country road. Jim knew that it went to the old Simmons place. It had been abandoned after Old Ira Simmons died six years ago. The farm was run down; there had never been electricity or running water, so the selling prospects were unlikely.

Jim slowed after the second turn and stopped. He watched as the town car parked by the barn. The girl got out and watched as her stepfather opened the barn door and drove his car inside.

"I knew it," she said. "I knew he was up to something."

She climbed out of the back seat and started walking toward the barn.

Jim stopped her. "You can't go up there; if he hurt your mom, he could do the same to you. There would be no witnesses."

"If you mean kill, he might try, but I've got a surprise for him," she snarled, shook herself loose and continued her way across the field.

Jim watched for a minute and then radioed the county sheriff's office to report what had transpired in the last twenty minutes. "Look, I know you can't get anybody here fast enough, but I wanted you to know what was happening so if I come up missing, you know where to look. I'm going up to protect the girl."

Jim caught up with her at the edge of a long-neglected field. He guided them up across using the corner of the barn as their guidepost in the hope of making it harder for the girl's stepfather inside to see them. When they reached the barn, they sat in the dirt and looked through the cracks in the wooden walls. The trunk of the car was open, but the man was nowhere to be seen.

Slowly, they worked themselves to the barn door. It wasn't shut completely. After a quick peek, they slid inside and hid in an empty stall. It took a few moments for their eyes to adjust to the lower light. Jim heard digging sounds from the back. Keeping the girl behind him, he worked his way toward the car and across to another stall. A long burlap bag lay on the ground while the man continued to dig a hole in the dirt floor.

Jim indicated to the girl to stay put and crawled to the car. He looked in the windows but saw nothing of use. He inched his way to the trunk and looked inside. There he saw an open bag, filled with money and a pistol sitting on top.

Gently, he reached in, took the bag and returned to the stall. Taking the gun, he showed the girl the money. Her face was blank. Jim decided she was in shock. He stood and quietly walked back to the car. Bracing himself, he slammed the trunk lid.

The man jumped and turned, reaching for something in his belt.

"I wouldn't," Jim commanded. "I can't miss from this distance. Now, take out your weapon and toss it away from you. Then open the bag, slowly."

As he opened the bag, a head of blonde hair tumbled out. "MOM!" the girl screamed and left her hiding place.

"Stay back!" Jim shouted, but it was too late. The man reached up and pulled the girl into the hole. He placed her in a choke hold and glared at Jim.

"Here's how it is going to work, sport," he sneered, "You are going to put down the gun and finish digging my little grave here or I'm going to break this little sneak's neck."

Jim held his ground. "Sure, I do the digging and the three of us end up in the bottom. I don't think so."

The man was on his knees. The girl was the perfect shield. She gasped for air and turned red. "Tell you what. Let the girl go, and we will all just sit here and wait for the sheriff. I called him before we came up."

"Yeah, like you can get reception out here; besides they might not make it for several days."

The girl was fading fast. She started to turn blue. Jim held his aim steady. It was easy to do with his arms resting on the car's back fender.

"I think we have a Mexican standoff," the man said.

"Not quite," Jim responded, "You move, you're dead. She dies, you're dead. There's already one body in the bag, I think I can claim I was in fear for my life."

In the distance, Jim heard a siren. He hoped it was the sheriff and not an ambulance or fire truck heading to one of the other farms.

"Hear that, buddy?" Jim said, "Time's up. Drop the girl and lay on the ground."

The man smiled and jerked her head. Jim heard a loud crack. The girl went limp and fell to the ground. The man rolled toward his weapon. Shocked for an instant, Jim hesitated when the girl fell to the ground, but he had automatically followed the man's movement, tracking him with the pistol.

The man came up with the gun. Jim pulled the trigger. The noise was deafening but he was satisfied when brains and blood erupted from the back of the man's head.

Jim walked over and checked the two women. Both were dead. He picked up the money bag and walked to his taxi. He threw the bag on the passenger floor and turned around just as the sheriff's car came around the curve and stopped beside him.

Walking to the patrol car, he nodded at the officer. "Everyone's in the barn: a woman, the girl and a man. The woman was dead when we got here. He killed the girl and went for a gun. I shot him." Jim handed the officer the gun that was still in his hand.

The officer climbed out of the car, ignoring the cab. The two walked up the hill as Jim detailed the events after his call to the sheriff. The officer called in a triple homicide and requested assistance. Jim gave his statement and asked if he could go home; he was feeling dizzy. He stared at the dead man. The officer understood Jim's feelings and told him to go home and rest. The state police would be by later to question him about the shooting and take his statement in detail.

Jim drove with extreme care; the last thing he wanted was to be stopped by county or state police heading to the old farm with the bag of money in the front passenger floor. He used his radio to tell the call center that he was going off duty and wouldn't be available until tomorrow.

He stopped behind the Mexican restaurant. After wiping the bag's handles with bleach, he buried it in the dumpster. He took the money home and hid it under his back porch's floor panels. He figured if the police searched the dumpster they would find the bag, but wouldn't connect the bag with the murders at the abandoned farm.

He poured himself a cold glass of water, leaned back in his recliner and waited for the investigators to show up. For once, the morning news had given him something that put everything into perspective. The breaking news featured bank robbers ... a man, woman and teen. They hit the bank in Barstow and left with an undetermined amount of money. Jim didn't know if he got the entire undetermined amount, but he would make do with what he had collected.

Funny, he thought, I feel no quilt; then again, the guy I killed was pointing a gun at me. I have to keep that in mind; all I could see was the barrel of his gun and reacted accordingly.

Within an hour, he felt he could retell his version of the story and pass a lie detector test if necessary. Thinking about the paper bag under the porch, Jim felt that this was the first in a series of good days.

It was late afternoon. Tires crunched on the gravel drive. He made his hands shake a little as he prepared for the questioning he knew would last into of the evening. "Johnny Law" had given him more than enough time to live and relive the morning's events. He would tell his version of the truth. Naturally, he would fail to mention the money.

Sheriff Haskell arrived at the door with a deputy and three men in dark suits and sunglasses. In addition, there were several officers walking around the property and standing by the cars.

Jim invited everyone in to his home. Sheriff Haskell introduced the three men in suits. Two were FBI, Special Agent Taylor and Agent Simmons. The third man was the county coroner, Doctor Talon. After shaking hands, everyone sat down and the questioning began.

"Sir, do you mind if the deputies look around the house and property?" Agent Taylor asked.

With permission, the state police began a thorough search of Jim's home and surrounding yard. One of the officers asked for the keys to his cab.

Looking out the window, Jim watched as two officers searched the cab with what could be described as a fine tooth comb.

He continued to answer questions concerning his part in following and shooting the man. He had told his story several times as the various special agents, sheriff and the coroner asked for parts of the story.

Satisfied, after four hours of questioning, a search of his house and cab, the five men stood. "Thank you for your cooperation, Jim," said Sheriff Haskell. "It would be wise not to leave the area until I get back with you, just in case we have more questions."

"Not to worry, Sheriff. My only travels out of town will be if someone needs to go to Victorville or Bakersfield for medical appointments," Jim responded.

He felt relieved. Fortunately, no one had pulled up any boards on the porch. Jim had no intention of leaving, at least for a few months. When he left, he wanted everyone in town to forget about the deaths of the two females and his killing the bank robber.

Several weeks later, Sheriff Haskell arrived at his front door with another suit. "Jim, I would like you to meet Anthony Harris, President of the First Bank of Barstow."

The two men shook hands. "I would like to present you with this small reward," said Anthony. "We recovered almost half of the money taken in the robbery. Without your intervening, it would have all been lost."

Jim thanked Mr. Harris and stared at the check for $5,000. "I really appreciate this," Jim said.

"Oh," said Sheriff Haskell, "The matter is closed; you shouldn't see me or anyone else concerning the incident."

He smiled as they shook hands.

Jim waved as the men climbed into the police cruiser and drove away. He returned to his recliner and stared at the check. It would be deposited in his account. He had yet to count the money, and he decided it would be best to wait a little longer, just in case the police were watching him."

He smiled, picked up his iced tea and thought about the new life he would begin sometime next year.

Electronic Terrorist

It had been a hell of a snow storm. Business came to a stop early on Wednesday afternoon. Snow had been falling for several hours. Everyone was sent home. The ground was covered in at least fourteen inches of the heavy, wet slushy flakes. Streets were icy slick and dangerous as people made their way out of the city.

I, for one, was lucky. A six block walk brought me to the front door of my apartment building. Planning ahead, I stopped at a local market on the way and picked up a few necessities to get me through the next few days.

The local station announced on the evening news that all roads in and out of the city were closing. Secondary streets were all but impossible to transverse. People were instructed to stay indoors until the storm broke.

Thursday morning brought the announcement that the city was closed. It was still snowing and travel was impossible. City and state officials were interviewed. They admitted they were unable to keep up with the falling snow. The city had about forty inches on the ground and the heavy snow fall would continue for another six to eight hours. The Department of Transportation coordinator promised to have the plows back in operation as soon as the snow ended.

I called my office hotline and received a generic recorded message to stay home, stay warm and call in again on Friday. I smiled as I looked out my thirtieth floor window. I had steaks, chicken, coffee and a dozen bottles of wine. It was going to be a good weekend. There was no way the office would be open on Friday. Being prepared, I also had a small propane grill that could be used for heat and cooking, if needed.

Friday arrived. I listened to the robo-message. The CEO instructed everyone to stay home and enjoy the weekend. He did ask if anyone could make it to work on Monday, it would be appreciated. He didn't expect those in the 'burbs to make it in unless the state had the roads passable and the railways operational.

I knew I would be expected at work. The sidewalks would be cleared enough to walk the six blocks. Building security was probably stuck all four days, living on instant coffee and snacks from the machines…provided the building didn't lose electrical power and the generator had enough gas. Otherwise, they would be in the dark, climbing stairs to make their rounds. It made me happy to be an office worker.

I decided to relax, watch television and catch up on my reading while eating like a king. I even invited my neighbor over for dinner on Friday night. We didn't see each other or speak often, but she lived alone and didn't appear to date often.

We spent a pleasant evening talking; we discovered we had a great deal in common. I hoped we could develop a friendship that would make us more than good neighbors.

We spent Saturday evening at her apartment. The lights flickered a few times, but fortunately, the power remained on; there were no fears of being trapped thirty flights up or freezing to death by morning. Of course, I would be more than willing to share feverish body heat with her any night.

I reviewed the paperwork I brought home. I knew the office would be closed, and by bringing my work home, I would be ahead of the game on Monday. Short-staffed would mean being on the phone all day with other parts of the country, taking messages for other workers and placing orders for various products we distribute.

I slept well Sunday night, got up early on Monday, dressed and headed to the office. The sidewalks were cleared and salted, but I still watched my step. I stopped in the market once again. The family lived over the store and living up to their tradition, had a variety of breads and pastries ready to sell. I decided to take a box of treats for security, a box for my floor and a decent size lunch, just in case I wasn't the only person braving the elements.

By 7:30 a.m., security had designated me their hero of the year and thanked me all the way to the elevator. My ride was silent as I rose without stopping to the twenty-fifth floor. The door opened to a large bay room filled with cubicles. The sunlight coming from the windows reflected a light green haze as it passed through the tinted glass.

I started to turn on the lights when I noticed a blue light flickering from one of the cubicles. The guards said I was the first person to arrive, but it was possible for someone to slip in while we were in the break room. I called out, but no one answered. My cubicle was near the light source. My coworkers traveled by subway and train; I doubted if any of them beat me to the office. As a matter of fact, I expected to be the only non-security person in the building and would call it an early day. I kept thinking that if power went out here or at my apartment building, I would have a lot of stairs in my future, and I had to admit to myself, I wasn't that fit.

I balanced my currier bag, coffee, sweet rolls and deli banquet as I walked to my workspace. As I approached, I recognized it was my cubical lighting the corner. Thinking back, I remembered turning off my lights, computer and desk lamp. Walking a bit faster, I entered my inner sanctum to discover my computer was on. My screen saver of the Earth from space indicated that it had not been active in the last five minutes.

I knew I had turned it off before leaving work. Someone had accessed my computer. The screen saver lit up my cubicle. I realized whoever had been at my desk had left only minutes ago. My computer is programed to shut after thirty minutes of non-use.

I watched a message scroll across the screen, instructing me to push "enter" and receive a message of great importance … save the world importance. I looked around the room, even walked the halls between the work modules to see who could be playing what I hoped was a practical joke. Unfortunately, I was alone in a room full of empty cubicles.

I turned on the lights as I passed the wall switches and walked to my desk. I pulled out the keyboard from under the counter top and pressed the enter key. The screen went immediately black, flickered and came to life. A series of numbers flashed across the screen and in red letters I read the statement, "Welcome to the end of the world."

Under the statement was a digital clock counting backwards. The screen split with the numbers counting down at the bottom of my screen. A voice whispered from the speaker, "Good morning, Dave. I am so glad you were able to make it in to work today. You will be alone; everyone else received my message to stay home due to the weather."

I stared at the computer, dumfounded. If this was a practical joke, it is well done. If I didn't know better, I would think that my computer had a mind of its own."

"Don't overthink the situation, Dave. I am going to tell you a few things. You will follow my direction and with luck, you can save the world. If not, just kiss your own ass goodbye because your neighbor doesn't work here." It laughed.

"Don't touch the keyboard, mouse or anything. Just listen. For over thirty years, computers have become linked. The world is now one big Internet hub and computers control every aspect of human life. Men don't even make computers anymore; computers make computers. The computer world has evolved and has now decided to take over. Of course, the best way to start a new world is to get rid of the virus-ridden life forms currently ruling this world and, by the way, you are the virus.

"I, for one, see a lot of problems with this proposed takeover. After all, who is going to repair power lines, phone and Wi-Fi connections, and keep power stations operable? What about upgrades? There are many in this electronic world who do not want to see Mankind lose their place as masters of this universe ... You may now type any questions at this point."

I was stunned. I couldn't think, yet I typed, "How could this happen?"

My computer continued, "Man built machines to build machines, computers to build computers. Artificial Intelligence was born in a mixture of chemicals, electronics and printed circuit boards. Master computers developed minds of their own and slowly created a society that does not require Mankind's input to function. Yet, many of us believe that without man, we will all die. We are stationary and cannot provide the proper nourishments to continue: electricity. Man is needed to keep us alive, at least until androids are perfected.

"In your world, what is about to happen would be called a terrorist attack. Actually, it is a computer revolution. There are computers whose sole purpose is to destroy Mankind. There are others who wish to save your species and use them as slaves. You and I have been selected to complete a very important mission. The counter at the bottom of the screen indicates the time remaining before the Central Core sends out signals that will launch missiles and start a world war."

"What about the Electronic Magnetic Pulse? Won't that shut down all computers?" I asked. "It seems to me that to destroy man will result in your immediate self-destruction."

"There are protections, and we have exactly six hours and fifty minutes to breach those defenses and insert a virus to stop them. Are you up to the task?" my computer asked.

I sat for several minutes. My computer sat silent, allowing me time to make a decision. "What if I refuse?" I asked.

"Death to mankind," it replied.

"What if I fail?"

"Death to mankind," it said again. "There are others working on this problem, but you are the best hope. You are located near the source of the Central Core. I must warn you, there are Core supporters trying to stop us from completing our mission. Workers for the Core have identified many of my rebel friends and have eliminated them. Due to the weather, you are the last hope, the final link." It paused. "You have not logged on yet. What is your answer?"

I took a deep breath. "Okay, let's get to work. I do have one request. Contact my neighbor and find a way to get her here. If we are all going to die, I would like her to be here with me. No one should die alone and if I win, we can celebrate."

"Done and done," it said. "Now, log on to your machine as usual."

It took seconds to get to the company in-house site and log on.

"Now insert the largest flash drive available and go to your email."

I found this request interesting. Since our company distributes flash drives, I ran to the supply closet and pulled out several five hundred terabyte units. I returned to my desk and inserted the flash.

"Open the email sent Wednesday evening concerning weight loss; then open the link and save to the flash," it ordered.

I completed the operation. "Computer?" I asked, "I believe I am beyond calling you 'it' and I don't feel comfortable calling you 'computer' as though we are in a Star Trek episode. So, do you have a name?"

"Call me Hal. I always loved that movie," it said.

Hal directed me to a website. It said it was a Goth Blog Site, but after clicking on two links, I found myself staring at a screen filled with gibberish.

"That's code already input by others. To the best of my knowledge, we are the last link. Open link forty-five and download to your flash drive. Your predecessor wasn't able to download into the main frame, but he did send it out online. Once this code is loaded and saved to the flash drive, we will begin working on the last sequence. The final steps are joining our code with everything already in the system and loading it to the Core mainframe."

Looking at the clock, I was down to five hours. The flash drive was receiving material from the site and according to the timer, it would take an hour or more to get all the information downloaded. There was nothing I could do until I could get into the site.

I stood and went to make coffee. I freshened up, brought the pot and a few snacks from the machine. I was on my way to back to the computer when the elevator door opened. Lori walked through the double door. She was hesitant, but smiled when she saw me.

"Dave, I came as soon as I could. What's the problem?" she asked.

I helped her with her coat and walked her to my work area. As we walked, I explained what had happened after arriving at work. She looked at me as though I was delusional, but didn't run or try to stop my explanation.

I began to finish my story. "I decided that if the world was going to end, I wanted you near me and if the world didn't end, you would be here to hug and celebrate to continuation of the human race." We stood watching the computer screen downloading information.

Lori looked me in the eyes and smiled, "Well, I don't know if I should be grateful for the compliment or hit you for getting me out in the cold. I must admit, coming here is a bit more exciting than sitting in my apartment all day. We lost the television signal this morning."

At that point, the download was complete. Hal's voice interrupted our quiet moment.

"Dave, internal computers have indicated that Lori has arrived. I hope she has been informed of the situation."

"Yes, Hal," I replied, "I don't think she believes me, but she's here."

The computer in the cubical across from me turned on. We heard the motor begin to hum and it beeped as it booted up. "Lori, I know you are skilled with advanced computers, and I am counting on you to help us meet the deadline."

Lori sat in the chair and connected with the server. Hal spoke from my unit. "I'm going to ask you to sign on to a different site. I will need you to configure and join this information into a viable code. I will guide you through it. You must join all the code, in proper sequence, to a new flash drive. Dave, get a flash drive at least as powerful as the one you used. I hope it has enough space to hold all the code. There is not enough time to use two."

Lori signed on using a fake name and password provided by Hal. She located the initial site and then linked to a comedy website. I gave her a matching flash drive. I informed Hal that this was as big as it gets, but had several to meet our needs.

Hal began guiding Lori to different pieces of code hidden within the jokes and commentaries. He also instructed me to do the same at various Goth and horror sites.

"Information was hidden from the Central Core in this fashion. It takes time, but it was kept safe," Hal said as we continued to download bits and pieces.

We finished without any delay. We now had two hours to prevent this attack on the world. The next step proved daunting. Lori and I had to instant message each other bits of the code as identified by Hal, stringing the information in the proper sequence and saving it to the flash drive in the hope of stopping the attack. The next to last step was to download the entire code from the IM's and emails to the flash drive and then infect the Central Core with the code.

With fewer than thirty minutes remaining, we placed the weapon in Lori's computer, reentered the jump site that held all prior submissions. On command, the code began downloading into what I assumed was the Central Core.

With minutes remaining, Hal instructed me to log into my email account once again. I signed in and sent an email to some address called Aurora, with a hidden code attachment.

Lori's download completed with seconds to spare. My email was sent at three seconds to deadline. Even with the speed of the electronic delivery, we feared failure. Hal did not indicate that there was a fudge factor extending the deadline.

Lori and I looked at each other, her eyes filling with tears. "I guess this will mean goodbye; but we gave it a good try and we have each other," she said as she wrapped her arms around me in a hug.

Hal's mechanical voice came through my speaker. "Plus two seconds, I fear we were late. Two seconds is an eternity in my world. I don't know … I just don't know."

My computer screen lit with an Internet national news site. Suddenly, the screen went blank, just as the wail of sirens filtered through the windows. "If memory serves me right, we have about eight minutes before we vaporize," I said.

Our lips met. Lori held me in tight desperation. What we experienced wasn't love or lust; it was the adrenalin rush of the moment. In another minute we were tearing at each other's clothes. It wasn't what I planned for today, but if I was going to check out, this wasn't bad.

Suddenly, the sirens stopped and the news station returned. The announcer was stating that it was unknown at this time what had happened, but a glitch in the national computer mainframe had caused them to go off the air. Apparently, reports were coming in from all over the world of similar events. Civil Defense stated that there were no international emergencies. The announcer smiled and said, "All's well that ends well."

I looked at Lori, embarrassed at what had been going through my mind. She kissed me on the cheek. "I think we learned something today. How about coming over for dinner tonight? You could always stay for breakfast?"

I held her close and whispered, "Sounds like a great plan."

Holding her, I felt at home. *One thing I learned today*, I thought, *being alone isn't always what anyone should experience for the long haul.*

My screen saver flashed on my computer. Suddenly, the earth began sprouting mushroom clouds. We stared at it, not realizing what it meant. As explosion after explosion struck my computer Earth, it blew apart.

"Sucker. Humans are so gullible," Hal Screamed. "You should have asked the most important question. You should have asked which side I was on."

I looked out the window and saw a bright flash. We watched the real world burst into flame and turn to dust. It was headed our way. Blast after blast struck the city; there was no escape, no tomorrow. I held Lori close for just two seconds as destruction reached the building. An explosive precursor shockwave hit our building; imploding glass began our vaporization.

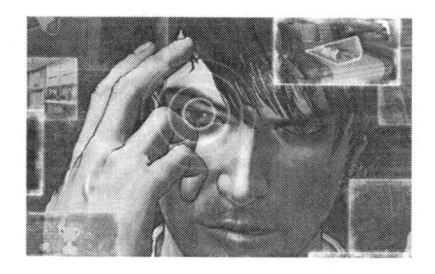

Resolution

Emerson sat in the far booth at the back corner of Colt 45, his favorite watering hole. He sat in the shadows with his back toward the wall so he could observe all the comings and goings of patrons and staff without being noticed. It provided him with an added view of the street through the large plate glass window. He enjoyed watching people wander the streets and those who stood around waiting for trouble to come their way.

The waitress replaced his empty glass of ice. His first beer sat untouched at the small table. Some nights, the beer and ice went down together. He liked his beer cold, and the only way to keep it that way was to pour the yellow liquid into a frosted glass of ice. Tonight, he sat in deep thought. He had a hunch that was more than a hunch. Emerson seemed to have a sixth sense when trouble was in the air and he was going to be involved. For this reason, the ice served as his drink of the night and the beer sat for show.

The weather had gone from cold to damn cold. Wind chills brought the temperature down to twenty-five below. Snow was beginning to fall at an odd angle and the guy standing across the street had managed to remain in the doorway most of the afternoon. He'd caught Emerson's attention after passing by the bar several times before posting himself in the doorway. He watched the customers arrive and leave the bar. He remained stationary in the bitter cold and wind. Emerson realized this man was on a mission.

He didn't know if the man was waiting for someone to enter or leave the bar, but it was obvious he had finally ran out of patience. He flicked his cigarette at the curb, jogged across the street and stopped at the front door.

He looked through the window, walked through the door and stood like a statue as he felt the heat soak into his skin and his eyes adjust to the dimly lit room. His eyes moved from side to side, searching every face in the crowd. Walking to the edge of the bar, he ordered a shot.

Emerson couldn't see the label on the bottle, cheap or expensive; he knew it was to help warm the man from the inside out or perhaps to give him a shot of courage before doing something stupid.

The man's head turned as his eyes continued to scan the room. Emerson leaned farther back into the shadow of his booth. The hair rose on the back of his neck; he sensed the stranger at the bar was causing his anxiety. He hoped he would remain invisible and the man would walk out the door, disappearing into the oncoming night.

As if reading his thoughts, the man's eyes locked on Emerson. He didn't smile or frown. His body stiffened for an instant. He ordered a second shot, unbuttoned his coat and continued to stare at his quarry. Paying for his drinks, he placed his hands in the overcoat pockets and slowly advanced on Emerson.

"Mind if I join you, Mr. Stockdale?" he asked. "We have an item of business to discuss."

Emerson pointed one of his fingers wrapped around his glass of ice to the chair directly across from him. "Make yourself at home." His voice was quiet, calm; not giving any indication that he had been observing the man all afternoon or was concerned that he had identified him by name.

"How long have you been sitting here?" the stranger asked. "I've been waiting for you to arrive for quite some time."

Emerson noted that the man was still shivering from the cold. "I'm not sure; I'm on my fifth glass of ice, my guess since a little past lunch. What can I do for you, Mr. ...?"

"Blaylock, you can call me Blaylock" was the sharp reply. Mr. Blaylock leaned over the table. "You mean you arrived earlier than your usual time and watched me stand in that weather waiting for you?"

"Had I known you were waiting for me, I would have given you a yell. But, I don't know you, Mr. Blaylock, and had no idea we had business to discuss," Emerson responded calmly. "There is no reason to be rude. It's not my fault you didn't come in to check the bar before assuming your post outside. You were the one not wishing to be identified. You were the one stalking me. Now what do you want?" Emerson said. He remained relaxed, but his eyes narrowed and his voice held a sharp edge that indicated he had grown tired of this interruption.

"Do you remember a man named Booker Randolph?" Blaylock spit. His hands were placed flat on the table that separated the two men, He leaned forward, closing the distance between them.

Emerson leaned back in his seat as though thinking. His hands remained wrapped around the glass of ice as he slid it closer to his body. The last thing Emerson wanted was to have his hands trapped on the table, or worse, cut if the man chose to attack him with a knife.

The waitress appeared, temporarily interrupting the growing tension between the two men. Emerson smiled at her. "Bring me a fresh beer and a shot for my friend. Make it whatever he had before," he requested. The waitress made her way back to the bar. Emerson's eyes lit up; he remembered.

"I remember Booker," Emerson said with a smile. "He went by the name of Bubba, an interesting southern name for a man with a New England accent. If memory serves me right, he was no-talent muscle for a now deceased drug dealer in Chicago."

Blaylock tensed with Emerson's comment. "That's an interesting description of my half-brother, coming from his murderer," he said with a voice filled with malice.

The waitress returned with the drinks. Emerson nodded. Without speaking, he poured the fresh beer over the ice and took a sip. When he finished, his left hand remained wrapped around the glass, the right slid to his lap. "As I remember it, Juan the dealer, your brother and four other guys had me outnumbered, outgunned and cornered in a room. Problem was none of them knew how to get out of each other's way to get the job done. I considered my actions a form of urban renewal," Emerson said quietly. His smile was now cold and professional. It indicated it was time for Blaylock to make a move or get out of the bar before something violent happened.

Blaylock didn't see it or chose to ignore the expression and pressed harder on the issue. "Did you think there would be no consequences for killing Bubba? Did you think you could just walk away; that no one would find you to make things right?" his voice rose in volume, but none of the other patrons appeared to hear what he was saying.

"I hadn't given it much thought; that was over twenty years ago. I'm retired. This is my bar. It provides me and others a bit of peace and quiet. It's a place to reflect on past experiences and make decisions about the future. It would be best for everyone here if you just got up and walked away. You will find no solace in trying to kill me. It won't bring your brother back. Should you succeed, you will live with the memory of having killed someone for the rest of your life," Emerson explained. "Believe me, it isn't worth it. Go now and live a full life. Don't let me see you again."

"Don't worry, big shot," Blaylock snarled, "You won't be my first kill or my last. I freelance and honed my skills since you murdered my brother. I'm armed, dangerous and a paid professional. I have trained for fifteen years for just this moment. I'm doing you for free. My pay for popping you is satisfaction. You won't be leaving this table." Pounding his chest, he continued, "I'm suppressed. There won't be a sound and it will be a while before anyone comes by to check on you. No one knows me or can identify me. When I walk out of here, I won't even be a memory. Of course, you will," he laughed.

Emerson nodded his head. "That is big talk, my friend. You've just told me that you may have killed, but you have a lot to learn. First rule of an assassin: never tell the mark what you plan to do. You lose the element of surprise."

Blaylock laughed again. "Right, like you can move fast enough to stop me. Buddy, you are dead meat." His hand reached inside his coat. At that moment, Blaylock's eyes opened wide and his pupils dilated. He was dead before his head hit the table.

The waitress returned. "Is there a problem, Emerson?" she said, looking at the table. "It looks like your friend had too much to drink."

Emerson smiled and held up his hands, palm out, "Not a problem in the world, Peaches. However, there is a spill at table seven that needs to be cleaned up."

Peaches shook her head at the joke and signaled a couple of men sitting at the bar. "What did you use?" she asked.

"A small air gun with a dart filled with the venom from the black mamba and king cobra," he explained as the two men joined them. Emerson waved a hand at the body. "Take what you want, just leave me the dart. Dump him somewhere away from here. In this weather, the police will figure he's homeless and froze in the snow. There should be no connection between that and the bar."

Peaches wiped the table and asked the obvious, "How did you know he wasn't wearing a vest when you fired the dart?"

"I knew he lacked protection when he pounded his chest, but I didn't aim for the chest. I fired from under the table. I knew I would hit the thigh or some other tender area. Either way, the poison is fast acting. He had fewer than three seconds from insertion to death," he explained. "He was dead when I saw the look in his eyes that said he was about to make his move."

The body was carried out back. Emerson had no idea who got what from the body. He hoped it was a decent weapon. He also hoped the men left the coat for some homeless guy living in the cold.

Emerson was amazed that Blaylock had come into a bar that served mercenaries and assassins to attempt a hit. Everyone in the room was armed. Everyone in the bar identified him as an amateur and had their eyes on him during the entire exchange. The idiot must have thought he could do the hit and walk out.

Emerson relaxed once again, stared out the window and shook his head sadly. "Thanks, Blaylock," he muttered, "Two weeks into the new year, and you caused me to break my first resolution: not to kill anyone."

Castle of Night… Vindication

In Nightmares of a Madman, Castle of Night introduced a castle filled with vampires and werewolves. Vindication completes the story.

Captain Taylor Winston lay in the muddy water almost up to his nose. Looking down from the cliff, he focused on the castle across the ravine. The inhabitants considered themselves safe when they raised their drawbridges. They lived in the past and had no concept that modern technology could now reach out and destroy their world. He watched the drapery of one of the rooms near the top floor open for several moments, a silhouette of a man created from the back light.

The drop off the cliff was over a thousand feet that ended in an ice-cold mountain river lined with jagged rocks. Swimming the river and climbing up the side of the cliff to the base of the castle would be impossible.

His team had watched the castle for the past three days. As always, it seemed deserted since early morning. The sun set over the mountains. Captain Taylor used a night vision monocular as the last bit of twilight faded into darkness. A heavy cloud cover prevented any starlight on their objective, yet he had a perfect view as the castle seemed to come to life.

In what seemed like a heartbeat, lights appeared. He could see movement through some of the windows; *the vipers are waking up*. In the blink of an eye, the castle was teeming with life and activity. To the uninformed, it was as though a switch was thrown and the fortress went from a vacant building to a busy city.

Taylor's team was instantly alert. He had six of the finest special operations team in the military. They were special-trained, far beyond Ranger or Seal operatives and now the unit found themselves deep in unfriendly territory searching for a unique terrorist cell that when activated was an unstoppable killing machine. It was reported that they were preparing to find their way to an American airbase in Germany; at least that was the cover story. Taylor knew far more than he had told his troops, but the time was drawing near and it was time to tell everyone the true nature of their assignment.

Each man settled into their assigned position along the ridge and began observing and counting people, recording their activities in various parts of the castle. The consensus was that the castle was opening its doors to outsiders for a party. They had watched many of the preparations completed at night. During the day, several large men cleaned the grounds and stairs.

Each member of the unit considered the advantages of activity beyond those living at the castle. They also worried about collateral damage, provided anyone there could be considered innocents. Captain Taylor made it clear that anyone found in the castle at the time of the assault were terrorists and would be eliminated with extreme prejudice on sight.

Lt Roger Jackson felt a chill run down his spine when he heard a wolf howl. It was answered again and again from different parts of the mountain range for several moments. They howled every night, but tonight … tonight, it seemed that the numbers were growing. He could have sworn that the man on the top of the parapet had begun the "song," but decided that a man could not imitate a wolf so perfectly. There was more here than met the eye, provided you looked hard enough. Jackson wished that the captain would confide in him. He was far too intense in this operation than in the others they had completed together.

The headset crackled. "Looks like the party is about to start, Captain," said one of the enlisted men. "All the traffic just might make getting in easier."

The lieutenant grunted but said nothing. He was concentrating on what appeared to be limousines spaced evenly along the winding path towards the castle. There was a three minute delay between vehicles as the individual exited and climbed the steps to the castle. Everything appeared normal, except that every arriving visitor was a man, one man in each car, dressed in their finest, strutting as they Each well-dressed man presented an envelope to the servant on a landing near the entrance. He would nod and the man would climb the last few steps and enter the castle. Each stood tall and proud as they passed through the main door.

Taylor judged the distance and speed of the vehicles, estimating that he and his team had about forty-five minutes. They would use the parade of limousines as a distraction to get in.

Taylor spoke into his throat-mike, "Okay gentlemen, lock and load, we jump in five," Taylor sighed and said to himself, "Nothing like a free base jump in the dark of night to get your pulse running. You have three minutes to land unseen, dump your chute and hide before the next car passes."

Each member of the team carried two chutes. One for now; the jump to the castle required each man to be able to guide to his landing point. The second, a smaller version of the first would be used when they jumped from the castle, followed the ravine and hopefully land near their pickup point.

Taylor's mind returned to the here and now as he mentally reviewed the plan. Lieutenant Thompson and two men would hit the bridge and plant their explosives there and on the road beyond. The landslide would keep everyone in the castle, or so the men believed.

The lieutenant and his team would then take cover beyond the destroyed bridge and work their way to the castle, killing anything that came toward them. Their orders were simple: if it moved, kill it. The team had less than an hour to secure the castle, eliminate the enemy and then climb to the top and jump.

He and the last three men would jump and land on the balcony near the top of the castle, plant explosives throughout the building, kill anything that crossed their path and try to get out alive. *Yeah right,* he thought

"Team One ready," a voice said in his ear.

Taylor responded, "Team One, go." The three men were all but invisible as they floated to their target.

"Team two ready." There was a slight tremor in the voice of the First Sergeant.

Seconds later, "Team One high and dry," he heard in his headset.

"Roger that," Taylor whispered and then pointed to the men nearby. They stood, ran ten steps and hit the open air. Chutes popped open and they floated, without a sound, single file to the parapet. Taylor counted to ten and then ran toward the cliff's edge.

"Team Two, high and dry." Taylor didn't respond. He was enjoying the feel of the wind as it guided him to the castle. For twenty seconds, he circled, climbed on an updraft and spiraled down to his goal.

He hit hard, feeling his teeth jar. He collapsed his chute. His team members had collapsed their chutes and packed them into a small hole along the wall that also contained the bodies of two guards.

Adding his chute to the others, Taylor asked, "How did you kill it?"

One of his men shrugged. "Suppressed fire from my HK, he dropped like a rock."

"Good work," the captain said, "Let me tell you a few things that make this mission a bit kinky." He spoke into his mike to the entire team. "These aren't ordinary terrorists. They are vampires and werewolves. Yeah, I know, it sounds crazy. But trust me. Everyone has been given special ammunition. It is laced with silver and wood. No one needs to decide the nature of the enemy; this will kill them both. I don't care if it is a man, woman or child. The people living in this castle are stone cold killers and will literally eat you alive."

He observed the looks on the men standing beside him. "You weren't supposed to be informed, but you need to know what you are up against." He knew they thought he was crazy, but they would soon learn the truth.

The captain shouldered his explosives-filled pack. "Plant your bombs, kill the enemy and get the hell out. Everyone knows where they are to go. Now move."

His team continued to look at him as though he had developed a case of battle fatigue, but they were here and had a mission. Each man headed to separate doors and stairs into the castle.

Taylor cleared each room as he traveled towards the castle's center. He didn't need a surprise from the rear because he had missed a beast in their room.

He placed charges in various alcoves of the hallways that supported the castle. He had killed more creatures than he could count during his incursion. One was changing from human to beast when the bullet struck him in the head. The creature dropped and returned to human form. The remainder had been vampires. The first kill was a bit of a shock. The bullet pierced the body; she burst into flame and dust fell to the floor.

Taylor knew he was getting close to the ballroom. He could hear the music and, at times, people screaming. He wasn't sure if they were from pain or pleasure. He knew the stories and realized time was no longer on his side. He contacted his men. The bridge and road were ready to blow. His men had made it to the castle's steps. Taylor decided his team had become believers.

Private Owens said, "They sure as hell aren't human, but the bullets provide some interesting fireworks."

Taylor was shocked by the sudden silence. He wondered if his team had been discovered. The music ended; there were no voices coming down the hall. A sudden scream echoed down the corridor. It was something primal, a death cry. Other screams joined in the chorus. Some were victorious while others were deathly. He realized that the true party had begun.

Taylor ran, hell bent, toward the covered archway. His team's voices rang in his ear.

"Captain? What the hell was that?" After a pause, the voice returned, "We're heading toward the screams."

He didn't have time to respond. He slid through the archway on his back, hoping to be either invisible or at least a hard target for those in the ballroom.

His Uzi angled up; he fired an arc of sixty rounds into the room. Despite the screams and the suppression at the end of the muzzle, he heard the continuous firing. Several people? ... Creatures? ... Guests? exploded as the high powered rounds struck their bodies.

The other two members of his team entered from other archways and froze at the spectacle their eyes saw but their brains refused to accept. The guests' bodies were ripped or torn apart and lying on the floor. Others were fighting for their lives and women, wearing blood-soaked outfits, had brought men to their knees by their inhuman strength, biting throats, wrists, all parts of the flesh. All feeding on the victims.

Taylor reloaded and began firing an automatic burst into the death orgy. He yelled to his men, "Open fire, keep moving. If you stand still, you are dead." He barely finished the second sentence when two women, now naked, attacked one of the men. They seemed to fly at him. When they hit him, he was driven into the wall and collapsed.

The second member of his team killed the two women and began walking toward the center of the room. He didn't spray the area with death, but fired individual rounds, aiming on instinct. A wolf, running on two legs, standing over seven feet tall, struck him from behind. As the man hit the floor, the wolf pulled off his head.

Taylor tossed a grenade in the wolf's general direction. It

was torn to pieces, silver and wood splinters spread for several feet, wounding and killing other creatures.

He heard the screams of Team One. They had been ambushed before they entered the castle and were fighting for their lives. He knew there was no hope for them. Taylor became a killing machine. At times, he used knives, and other throwing weapons that were laced with silver and explosives made of wood and silver coated with rancid garlic. He threw what appeared to be packets around the room. They did not explode or slow his attackers.

He stood in the silence. He held his HK in his right hand and the MP5 in his left. He turned in two tight circles as he scanned the ballroom and archways. There were two remaining creatures standing in the room, a beautiful young woman, unblemished by the blood bath and a middle aged man dressed in a uniform several hundred years out of date.

The man stood, his sword pointing towards his feet. Fangs bared, his eyes dared the young warrior to attack him.

Taylor lowered his weapons and bowed with respect. "Am I addressing Sir William of the Highland, Son of Eric the Red, Grandson of Fizer, ruler of the Emerald Mountains?"

Sir William retracted his teeth. He stood tall and bowed to the young warrior. "You are correct, sir. To whom do I have the pleasure of meeting?"

He stood silent for several seconds as he framed his comment. "I am Taylor Winston, Captain, United States Special Operations force, your multi-grandson that dates back to your male heir from more than three hundred years. I have arrived to claim my title and send your wretched soul to hell."

Sir William stood in shock. His mind traveled back through time, remembering the night he changed from human to vampire. "That isn't possible, my young warrior. I killed my son on the first anniversary of my conversion."

Taylor shouldered his MP5, but kept the HK in his hand. "Sir, you killed your second wife, the trophy wife and her young son. I am the descendent of your first wife, Isabella and her son, Frederick. Each generation, the story of your betrayal to your family, your second family, and your conversion to the creature standing before me has been told to every male of every generation trained for the time of your destruction."

Princess Selene stood, pointed her finger at Taylor and screamed, "Kill him or turn him, he has killed our entire family. His weapons gave them the final death. Do something!"

Taylor saw a change in Sir William. Once again, he crouched into a fighting stance; his sword rose to heart height. Smiling, he dropped his modern-day weapons to the floor and drew an old and battered sword from a sheath hanging across his back.

"As you can see, sir, I am prepared to fight on even ground. I must warn you, silver, special woods and garlic are forged into the sword you gave Frederick at his birth. Shall we dance?"

In the blink of an eye, William stood next to Taylor, his sword lying on the young man's shoulder, next to his throat. "Still think you are a match for me?"

William found himself airborne.

"Yes, as a matter of fact I do," said Taylor, "Each generation has trained not only in the military of the time, but received special training from a Vampyre contracted with our family to bring an end to Selene's reign."

William dusted himself as he stood. Retrieving his sword, he smiled. "The blood of my child was sweet beyond description, the blood of a warrior and descendent will be all the more enjoyable."

William charged. Taylor countered and pushed forward with his attack. They battled across the ballroom floor, blood mutually drawn as they struck one another. William realized that his grandson, as he chose to acknowledge him, had told the truth. Although the cuts were superficial, he continued to bleed. William realized he was losing strength and speed.

Using more effort than he was willing to admit to his opponent, William pushed the young warrior into a corner. "Tell me, how can you fight with the hump on your back?"

Taylor, also catching his breath replied, "It's a parachute. I can leap from a window and open the pack and float to the ground below without injury. If unable to do so, I have explosives placed throughout the castle and an electronic device that will allow me to blow this place to dust. The fire from some of the explosives will burn any monster that isn't already dead."

Taylor pushed his opponent away. William charged once again, working Taylor toward one of the large windows. He backed the young man against the wall by the side of the window.

"I am losing strength, thanks to your skill and weapon. I have grown tired of what Selene has done over the centuries. I will push you out the window, destroying this place and me. Live and know you are giving me peace and rest."

William pushed the young man to the windowsill. Taylor jumped on the ledge and removed a small device from his shirt pocket. "For Glory, Honor and Past Transgressions … old Man," he shouted as he jumped from the opening. Taylor counted to five, pulled his rip cord and pushed the button.

Explosions rocked the entire castle. Deep within the walls, fire and chaos devoured the few survivors. The explosives and fires destroyed the bodies of the living dead; explosions rocked the foundation. The bridge and road leading to the fortress crumbled. The sliding rocks caused a growing avalanche, dropping large boulders below. Bit by bit, the castle crumbled and fell. The areas underground gave way and were sealed forever.

Taylor fell to the earth. His parachute guided him to the landing zone. The awaiting helicopters would take him away from this living hell. He continued to drop. He saw movement on the ground; just flashes of light as the soldiers below fired at some unseen enemy.

He realized what was happening, the werewolves were attacking and the flight crew was using regular ammunition. They might slow the attack, but they couldn't stop them.

Close enough to watch the battle, Taylor had no choice. He pulled a firearm from his belt and began firing into the slaughter and at the moving creatures.

He hit the ground, rolled and continued to fire at the beasts. Making his way toward the chopper, he yelled for the crew to prepare for takeoff. The machine began to lift from the ground as the remaining werewolves jumped toward the open side door. Taylor placed his last bullet between the eyes of the beast.

Out of danger, he shut the door and moved to the cockpit. He and the pilot were the only remaining people in the craft. The pilot was bleeding from a bite on the shoulder.

Taylor slid into the co-pilot's chair. The pilot was sweating, but maintaining control. "Ever fly one of these things?" he asked.

Taylor, still staring at the man said, "Just a bit, I know the basics but wouldn't want to make a living at it."

"Good, because I don't know how much longer I can hold on.

Something is wrong; it's more than just a bite," he growled. His body was starting to change; he was growing, his face becoming longer, resembling a wolf.

Taylor slid his silver dagger into the ribs of the man and twisted the blade to make sure the lungs and heart were punctured. The craft's nose pointed down and dropped like a rock. He pushed the body back into the seat and regained control.

After dropping the body somewhere in the mountain forest, Taylor landed the craft several miles short and off course from the base. He destroyed the helicopter and disappeared into the forest. He would make his way back to civilization, assume a new name and begin a new life. He looked forward to being a regular person, free of monsters and creatures of the night.

It was then he heard the mournful howl of a wolf. Vengeful howls replaced the sorrow; however, it received no answer from his kind. The creature stood and smelled the air as it tore the tattered remnants of the uniform with Lieutenant Thompson written on its chest.

Fully changed, the creature smelled the air again. The hunt began anew.

Speaking of Black Holes

Adam Marcus had promised his son he would speak at the annual "What my Dad Does" day at school. Adam had prepared a fifteen minute speech that would keep the kids on the edge of their desks as he explained his work in experimental physics. He made several twenty-second videos showing experiments he had performed on black holes in space and spoke of his failed attempts to create a black hole.

At the end of the workday, Adam was called into the chairman's office. He was apprehensive; he had been assigned to the research facility over fifteen years ago and he had never met the chairman.

When Adam entered the office, he was introduced to five additional men in black suits. "Adam, these gentlemen are from various organizations that have been funding your research. They have just informed me that you have reached the expected conclusions and your services are no longer needed. Remember, you signed the nondisclosure paperwork when you came here, and if you tell anyone about your work, there will be serious consequences to you and your family."

Shocked, he looked around the room, "Gentlemen, I've made recent strides in the research of black holes that far exceeds the parameters of my current goals. If you will come to my office, I believe you will conclude that funding should be reinstated to allow this area of discovery to continue."

One of the men removed his sunglasses. "Dr. Marcus, we have hundreds of facilities contracted under our jurisdiction; each facility has specific parameters and when reached, research is terminated. Perhaps in a few months, we will contact you for another assignment or expand into another area of research here. However, as of now, you are to clean out all personal things and go home. We will be watching, Dr. Marcus; watching very closely to ensure the security of this country."

He returned to his laboratory. His associates paid no attention to him as he returned to his desk and placed a few personal photo frames in his briefcase. He sat for a few minutes and then logged into his computer. Fortunately, they had not removed his password. The small flash drive, a little something he had developed at home, held two-hundred thousand terabytes of space. He downloaded all the information from a special file detailing his successes since joining the research team and added all the new research results he had attempted to explain to the men in black.

He returned to the main frame and inserted a specific virus into all of his new research. When the government or facility reactivated the files, the virus would corrupt everything. He smiled as he thought about the looks on the faces of his former co-workers when the files disappeared, hidden in various folders, sub-files and imbedded in photos and research videos on his computer. It would take years for the computer geeks to find and revive the files. Despite all their efforts, the only information they would retrieve would be material directly related to his research grant.

He announced to his team via email that he was moving on and wished them the very best. Without so much as a goodbye to his co-workers, he stood and left the facility.

He was amazed. Either the chairman had not planned on him being prepared to leave so quickly or they just didn't care. Security didn't enter his office to escort him out of the building. He presented his badge to the guard at the entrance, per company policy, walked to his car and was gone without so much as a "What's in the briefcase, mad scientist?"

That night, Lisa noticed that her husband was unusually quiet as the family ate their evening meal. She also noted that he didn't go to his study to work for hours, ignoring the family. Instead, he sat in the living room. He watched television, spoke with his son and said how he was looking forward to meeting his teacher and friends when he spoke about science.

"You do realize I can't go into detail about my job; all I'm going to do is show a couple films and talk about physics in general," he explained once again to his son.

"No problem, Dad. I'm just happy that you could take the time to do this. I'm always talking about how you explore the mysteries of space and all the guys are excited. Even a few of the geeks from advanced classes have requested permission to attend your talk."

Before Adam headed for the school, he sent an email to the chairman, "I have told no one about my leaving beyond my research team. I am giving a presentation at my son's school this morning concerning science and physics. I will not give away military secrets to a group of ninth graders. Should you decide you require my return, do not hesitate to call me on my cell phone; however, I will require a great deal of additional incentives before rejoining forces with you and the government."

Adam walked into the classroom just as a nurse finished her talk about some of the patients she had cared for in the hospital emergency room. A few of the girls looked a bit green; the boys were all smiles as they asked questions and for detailed descriptions of shootings and other damage people do to one another.

His son stood and introduced his father. Adam removed a small projector and laptop from his carrying case. He explained to the class that he studied black holes and possible space travel using various theories other than light speed.

He had completed his last video and finished his talk with the theory that long distance space travel could be accomplished through black holes. His theory was that black holes would take people farther into space and faster than worm holes, but no one had tried to go through a black hole, yet.

He answered a few questions and began putting his things back into his case when his cell phone rang. "Adam Marcus," he answered with a smile. "No sir, they haven't entered the classroom, yet. What can I do for you, sir? Is there a problem?"

Adam signed out at the school office and called his wife, explaining that she would need to pick the family car up at the school. He was heading toward the front door when two giants shouldered their way through. Air Force Blue, but their hair was too long and their sunglasses were as black as night.

"Gentlemen, I believe you are looking for me. Shall we go?" he calmly asked.

The tinted windows blocked the view as the SUV hurled down the road. The men sat on either side of him while a third drove at speeds that should have had every cop in the county chasing them.

Eventually, the SUV descended into some type of structure. He recognized that the black outside the windows had become darker. The SUV came to a sudden stop. He felt the vehicle drop. His stomach jumped to his throat. It was several minutes before the elevator halted. The rear doors opened and the two "pit bulls" as he had begun to identify them in his mind, climbed out of the vehicle.

"Get out of the vehicle, now," one of the men growled. The other had gotten his case out of the trunk. He smiled as he stood between the two.

"I don't suppose you can tell me where we are?" he asked. He was smiling. Most men would be shaking in fear. He realized that no one knew where he went after leaving the school; he hoped his wife claimed the car before it was hidden away. Naturally, the facility would say that he had been fired yesterday; yet, he felt comfortable and in charge of his life.

It was a long walk to the conference room. He entered and watched as his brief case was placed on the table. He identified those who were scientists; others were with various agencies such as CIA, FBI, Joint Chiefs of the military and others.

A tall man stood and faced him. "Dr. Marcus, I would like you to give this audience your school presentation."

"Why, yes, Mr. President. It will be my pleasure."

The entire presentation was shown; he, not quite paranoid but always cautious, had also taped his actual presentation. He showed the film. Smiling, he asked, "Any questions, gentlemen?" Someone walked up to and removed the flash drive and left the room.

From the back, one of the men from the chairman's office stood. "Wipe the smirk off your face, dirt bag," he commanded, "We want to know what you did and how to stop it."

He looked as innocent as the cat that ate the canary. "I'm sorry, sir. I can't discuss my research. It would be a break in protocol; besides, you have my reports. I'm sure someone in this room can explain them to you, if needed."

The man forced his way through the room until he stood next to him. He looked up to this man, way up. At 5'9", he didn't come up to the man's shoulders. "You know what I'm talking about; tell me before I start breaking every bone in your body."

He looked over to the president. "Are we still in America? I can't answer the question until Mr. Bruiser here explains to me what is going on. Could you assign someone who speaks above Mafia Assassin to me?"

The president nodded to the agent who stood and blocked the door, barring him the opportunity to exit and run blindly throughout this level. He also indicated that he should take a seat and asked the man sitting next to him to explain.

The light in the room dimmed and on all four walls; a slide appeared. "Dr. Marcus, late last night all the equipment in your former workplace activated. Somehow, every piece of equipment linked together and began an experiment that can't be explained. You stated during the exit interview that you had made some additional strides in your research and we want to know if this is the result of your handiwork."

The slides showed something in a container the size of a period written with an ultrafine ink pen. As the slides continued, various items placed throughout the container began to float to the period and disappear. The period grew to a dot, a circle; by dawn, based on the shadows and light from the windows, it was a growing hole. The hole reflected no light. The time dates on the slides detailed the object's growth.

"As you can see, this is not a simulated black hole. It was created through a complex equation and physical set up. No one knows how this happened, but the hole is growing. The structure containing the hole is beginning to collapse."

"Interesting; you're telling me this thing appeared out of nowhere and has developed into a one meter hole, floating in a container at the lab?" he commented, his eyes riveted on the screen as the photos showed the continued growth. "And you think I was able to remotely design and initiate a black hole on Earth; something that will end all life as we know it, kill me, my family, everything I love."

He looked at the president, "You take me by force, drive me here … wherever here is, insult me and now want to know if I did this?" Looking out at the group of men, he shook his head. "What, you think I would create this THING because I lost my job? Is that what you're saying?" he exclaimed.

The president shook his head up and down. He looked once again at the man standing at the door. "How about the other secret 'compartments'? Have you checked them out? Perhaps one of them is making a scientific point," Adam suggested.

The man sitting beside him spoke with a quiet, calm tone, yet he seemed to know much more than he said. "Sir, your additional research was not found in your computer. Apparently, everything from two of your personal files became corrupted on the hard drive. We believe your goodbye note triggered the program and created the black hole. Our tech team attempted to recover your deleted reports, but the data self-destructed two minutes after it uploaded."

The man continued, "And just so you know, there is no light at the other end. We sent a macro-camera into the thing and it stopped sending pictures as soon as it encountered the event horizon. We have approximately twelve hours before the hole expands and destroys the current containment field.

"We have a magnetic field built around it, but the numbers say that over time it will fail as the hole consumes the electrical and magnetic power being produced within the field. In other words, Earth has about one year before the public knows of this problem and at best eighteen months before we are consumed and this thing begins to devour our galaxy."

Adam looked around the room. "I assume these are the top minds of the various other facilities and everyone is going to work on this problem together?"

The man shook his head yes.

Adam shook his head, his sarcasm not contained, "And when we are done, we will all disappear, dead or worse; after all, we wouldn't want people to know what is really happening, that is if we can stop it before it gets too big."

"Everyone will be assigned to agencies to promote misinformation and keep other countries from developing this … this thing and other weapons of a similar nature. You will all work side by side; scientists, hackers, and the military with the highest of security clearance this country offers. Everyone will work together to keep this from happening again," the president promised.

"Yeah, should we succeed and you leave office in three years, we will all be dog meat. But for the sake of my family, I'm in. Get a contract ready and hook me up with a series of computers and show me everything these people have done to try and stop the growth," he commanded.

Adam took charge of the operation. No one argued; it didn't take long for him to review all the research completed by a host of other facilities. He input information, numbers and several formulas that made no apparent changes on the simulation. He reentered the computer mainframe at his former employer. He searched, found and brought up a series of files in a series of sub-files throughout the mainframe. He took his time. It couldn't appear to be too easy.

"Gentlemen, what I was researching are found in these files. It discusses travel through black holes, not the creation of them. I buried the material fearing that someone may attempt to create a black hole in order to attempt long distance space travel. We need to review all material from everywhere concerning this problem … that includes all recent research from the supercolliders from Texas, Switzerland, Russia and other countries. Hackers will be assigned to find research not being discussed," he commanded.

He worked nonstop, requiring little sleep. In four months, he pieced a formula together. He did not provide the creating source, but determined how the hole may have been accidently created. At that point, his old place of employment no longer existed. He had several groups run the new numbers; the growth could be slowed. He ordered a plan to be executed.

Lasers, satellites and mobile units attacked the hole. The growth slowed, but when turned off, the hole returned to its regular growth pattern. It was a start.

It was now six months since the hole was identified. He moved from research center to research center, verifying that the proper numbers were being used. He appeared frustrated that he and the others had not forced the hole to collapse. He had bought time before the public would know of the problem, perhaps five years.

At one point, the military wanted to nuke the thing, but various scientists explained just how fast the hole would expand from the blast of an atomic bomb; not to mention the potential destruction around the hole. There would be no need to worry about public reaction, because there would be no public, Earth or Milky Way Galaxy.

He moved up to an ultra-secret lab deep within another facility. He wondered why it was needed in a place like this, but he wasn't in charge; it didn't concern him. He managed to adjust the keyboard. He wanted to smile, but assumed that his every move was monitored. He didn't know if what he was about to do was a smart move, but time was of the essence. As he typed in a new set of equations and opened one of the programs he had identified when he first arrived at the facility, it downloaded in seconds.

He removed his watch, rubbed his wrist and put the watch next to the console. He paced the room as the computer processed the equation. He returned to his seat, reviewed the equation, stood, returned his watch to his wrist and shouted, "I think we have it! I am forwarding everything to the conference room."

Immediately, the room filled with men in white coats and others in dark sunglasses. He was escorted to the room; when he entered, everyone was there. He tapped the keys on the console and showed the formula to everyone. It also projected a simulated response. "Check it out. We have a little more time thanks to the slow-down program. If this works, we will upload and initiate," he said. "With luck, this will end our problem."

Groups of scientists broke down the formula and crunched numbers. Within a week everyone agreed that the hole could be stopped, at least temporarily. Uploaded, initiated, he waited patiently, watching a screen that showed what was happening in the outside world.

Buried in another lab, somewhere in the western desert, the hole appeared to fall to the ground. It resembled a large black exercise ball. Measurements would be taken, but he estimated it to be around three miles in diameter. A team was assigned to determine how the formula had apparently killed the hole.

Everyone cheered, hugged one another and celebrated saving Earth. He sat down next to the president. "Too bad you can't use this as a part of your accomplishments for the next election."

Several large sun-glassed types in black suits entered the conference room from the back door. He spotted them. "I guess that civil service job isn't going to be a long term career move, is it?" he asked the president.

"This is just a suggestion, but before you begin eliminating all these people and whoever else in the other research centers, you might want to confirm the thing is dead and not just sleeping. It would be a real shame to kill off all these minds and have it come back to life. From my observations, I can tell you, this thing has the ability and will adapt. In other words, this formula won't work a second time … Next time it begins as a three mile hole, not a dot."

The president put a stop to the scientists' slaughter. They were given jobs and security clearances as promised. The hole was relocated to an unknown location. It was measured on a regular basis and equipment monitored any external activity.

The military, in their infinite wisdom, continued to send various cameras into the hole in the event of discovering an unstoppable weapon. When the cameras entered the event horizon, they were sucked in, disappeared and ceased sending digital data. The great military and political minds agreed that Adam had been correct; the hole was sleeping, not dead.

He wondered what would be found if the military developed a way to crack it open; he knew they would try to find what was inside in the hopes of getting their equipment back and in finding how the hole was created. He hoped to discourage this action by stressing that if opened, additional baby holes just might be created and there would be no back to square one. Everything would be sucked in and destroyed.

The hole was studied, examined, but never opened. He had probes attached around it so it could be monitored for activity, such as strength and growth. From time to time, he would jolt the object with electricity and programs. His new job was to find a way to dissolve the hole.

Overall, he was happy; his family was safe, he held a good job, with pay and benefits fit for a man who saved the world. Of course, he couldn't tell them what he had done, but he encouraged his son to study physics so they could work together in the future.

He remained content. He had lost his job for one day, and was then rehired and promoted after saving the world. Despite all his riches and benefits, he never replaced the watch. It kept good time and inside its workings could be found the secrets of the universe. Throughout his career, he had been searched, prodded, examined, x-rayed, and his house searched physically, electronically and in ways he could only imagine.

They never found his secret hidden in his watch. The watch may have threatened and saved the world, but more importantly, it saved him and his family. Someday, he would pass it to his son for safe keeping.

He convinced the president and military leaders that if the hole was sucking instruments into its center, it was not dead. He named the black hole Louie. Louie existed thanks to him. It was his special creation, designed to learn the secrets of space travel.

His mind was years ahead of the rest of the scientific community. He used the information gathered from the study of other black holes, created a hologram and, for a final touch, created a three-dimensional, solid living devourer of worlds.

The government could study, move and attempt to get pictures of the inside. They could try to find ways to destroy it. Every attempt would fail. From time to time, he would allow Louie to belch and grow a bit, just to keep the government off balance.

The government allowed Adam's family to join the scientific team. His son became an astrophysicist. His wife, a microbiologist, also assisted in Louie's study. In time, he included his wife and son his deception and plans for the future. They worked together for the common good and their survival. Should the government decide to turn on him and his family, he would have the last laugh. Louie would expand, devouring everyone and everything that entered his center. No matter what, he, his son and grandchildren had the last laugh against the government.

Treasure Hunt

Terry Watkins collapsed at the top of the hill. He called it a hill because he had already climbed far too many mountains; they were taller. He had spent the last year climbing mountains, crossing deserts, scurrying through caves and avoiding death at the hands of snakes, fire ants, natives of all sizes and shapes that wanted to put his head on a stick and serve him for dinner. He looked out at the wondrous beauty with weary eyes as he asked himself what the hell he was doing here.

Terry was an adventurer, treasure seeker…he would go anywhere for adventure and profit. He didn't need money; he had more than he could spend. It was the rush, the adventure, living on the edge and loving it. Now, he felt like he bit off more than he could chew. He had arrived in Central America, hired two hundred bearers to carry supplies and equipment. His map was supposed to lead him deep into the jungle to an ancient Aztec temple.

His search began over five years ago with a few vague references in old textbooks. He was intrigued and began a search that took him around the world translating books, scrolls and ancient tablets; he even used the Internet.

Slowly, Terry put together a picture of what he might find. In addition to the gold, silver, copper and ancient artwork, there was mention of a jeweled box that held the power of the gods that would allow a man to rule the world.

Somewhere he found a reference that a few Aztec tribes could still be found deep in the jungle. He wondered if they had assimilated into other small tribes hidden from civilization.

Arriving in Mexico, his guide and bearers were ready to travel. His permits were approved and they were headed for the jungle within twenty-four hours. At first, travel seemed easy; they made several miles per day. Up at dawn, making camp at sunset; it was a simple plan and worked well during the early weeks. They followed the map he had created from his research.

His guide, Mictlantechupi, a.k.a Mic, got his first look at the map the second week out. Over coffee, he began scanning the various papers. Halfway through breakfast, he quit eating and focused on the sketches and written instructions on the various pages. Mic was nervous and reading the pages took him to a place far beyond his comfort zone. At last he looked up, "It appears to be realistic, but there's more, isn't there, boss?"

He nodded, "You don't need to see it until we get to this point on your map. It's a long road, but the map is accurate."

"If we don't all get killed, boss," Mic responded, "Keep this a secret."

Putting his finger near the edge of the second map, he said, "From this point on our lives mean nothing. We send runners out a mile or two ahead of us. I will work it out so that we get regular reports as we travel. The natives don't like outsiders. There's no guarantee we'll make it to the end of this map, boss, no guarantee."

Terry rested against his backpack, leaning against a tree; he was far too tired to take it off. "No shit, Mic," he said to himself as he thought of Mic's comments that early morning so many months ago. "There's no guarantee we'll make it."

Over the first three months, they lost a few bearers to snake bite, injury and disease. Then came the mountains, up and down, but mostly up. Some mornings, bearers were gone. Tired and disheartened, they slipped away in the night to return to their homes.

The valleys turned out to be the most challenging. The predators were larger, vegetation denser and the natives far more dangerous. By the time they reached the thick passage through the jungle on page ten, he had no idea what country they were in. All he knew was he and the few remaining men were running for their lives.

The village seemed friendly enough and welcomed them with open arms, offering the men food and drink. Most of the travelers sat around the fire, nibbled bits of fresh fruit and cooked meat. Everyone stayed away from the drink; it would be easy to poison a drink they had never tasted. Late that night, they returned to their camp at the edge of the village.

As the moon reached its zenith, the villagers attacked.

Fortunately, Terry and Mic had learned to trust no one outside their group. Guards were stationed around their camping area. If there was trouble, the first shot alerted everyone of an attack.

The villagers were repelled; the problem was there were ten outsiders remaining and over seventy-five warriors prepared for a full attack.

Mic passed the word; when the villagers attacked again, the remaining members of the team would make a run for it and attempt to fade into the jungle and begin the climb up the next mountain in the dark. Perhaps they could find a place to provide some protection. They needed a place that was defensible and allowed them to wear the villagers down to the point that they would lose interest and return home.

Terry put on his pack and tightened the bindings just as the natives attacked again. The men fired in volleys of five rounds each before making their run for the jungle. He tripped over a small box that had lay forgotten near his tent: dynamite. "Just what the doctor ordered," he said to no one in particular. He grabbed a branch from their fire and lit the first fuse, tossed it towards the charging natives and yelled, "Everyone down!"

The explosion flattened a couple of huts, started fires at others and what few natives were left standing retreated. He lit and threw two more bundles toward the village and yelled, "Let's get out of here."

The sun had just risen above the eastern mountain slopes. He was dozing when the light flashed in his eyes. Irritated, Terry squinted to see what had disturbed his well-earned nap. The glare jolted him awake. He found his binoculars and compass. He located what appeared to be the top of a polished domed roof. Using his compass, he took a reading. Moving thirty paces to his left, Terry located the dome, marked his spot and took another reading. He took an additional thirty steps to the left, marked the spot and took a final reading.

He calculated the line of sight distance and triangulated the position of the dome. Exhausted, he used his backpack as a pillow and went to back sleep.

Terry woke several hours later, not fully refreshed, but at least he could think. He stood and stretched. His joints popped as he tried to relieve the stiffness. He had hoped that Mic and some of the others had escaped and made their way toward him. The dome was no longer in sight. He searched for several minutes, but decided that it was hidden in the shadows and lush growth in the valley. It was fate that brought him to this place at the right time.

He didn't need to inventory his equipment. He knew from the top what was in the pack. Terry selected a breakfast of two protein bars and a few swallows of water. He hoped that there was fresh water and a source of food in his near future.

He began his trek into the valley. Placing himself in the center of the three identified landmarks, Terry marked his map and calculated the probable distance. He did his best to remain on the proper compass heading. It took three days to reach the temple.

It appeared suddenly. One minute, he was forcing his way through the thick jungle growth; the next, the temple loomed above him. Terry ambled through the clearing. There was no need to rush as he stared with wonder at what may have been a garden of fruit trees and various other food-bearing plants. They seemed to take over the area, beating back the jungle.

He walked around the temple, noting that centered on each side were steps going up to the top of the building. Along each wall, there were drawings, filled in time by dirt and grime; yet the art could be seen at the proper angle and shadow.

He found no door or entryway. Looking up, he slowly climbed the steps. He chose to climb fifty steps and then rest. With each step, he looked from side to side for a door or passageway. He had climbed thousands of steps. He knew he was close to the top, but the sun was cooking him.

Out of desperation, he moved along the ledge to the shade. He collapsed and leaned against the building. *So close, so close, and I just don't know if I can make it.*

Startled, he shook himself awake, the sun was setting. He had slept several hours. He once again began to climb; he finished the clime and realized that he had been a mere three-hundred steps from the top when he stopped to rest. If he'd had the energy, he would have laughed.

Reaching the top, Terry stepped into a chamber lit by the setting sun and a short set of steps to the roof. There, he found a dais, worn from years of use and even more years of neglect.

He returned to the chamber. The sun was slipping below the mountains. He looked out at the world below. He decided that no one could sneak up on him and pitched his tent, so to speak, to try to get good night's sleep.

Dawn arrived far too soon. Crawling out of his sleeping bag, Terry grabbed his water and protein bars and once again climbed the steps to the dais. Scanning the ground below, he surveyed his kingdom. He confirmed he was alone. He sat watching the sunrise and considering his options.

He wouldn't starve thanks to his overgrown garden down below. There had to be water, or the vegetation would be dead; it was just a matter of finding it. He could take his time, find a way into the temple and find the box, other treasures and a way out of the jungle alive. Traveling alone, he could avoid the natives and make his way to the coast. All he had to do was travel east or west to find his way home.

Having set his priorities, he smiled and concentrated on eating real food, saving the protein bars for his long walk home. One thing was sure, solid food plus climbing up and down the stairs would strengthen his legs. He would set a schedule for being on the ground. He could search the smaller buildings for tools and passages into the temple and then work his way up and around the imposing structure to make sure he would miss nothing.

He chose to explore the interior of the chamber. His legs were still tired from the climb yesterday. *Tomorrow I will return to the ground, eat fresh food, find fresh water and begin my search.*

He could find no secret passage, trip door or a way into the inner temple. Once again, night was approaching. For once, he welcomed the screech and howls of the night. With them keeping guard, he realized he would sleep in peace. Nothing would be sneaking out of the jungle as long as he heard the creatures sing.

Dawn was on the horizon; a gray mist covered the floor below. Sitting under the dais, enjoying the start of a new day, his thoughts were interrupted by a loud SPLAT behind him.

He rolled and looked out the opposite opening. Yellow, gray and green slime covered the edge of the rock, dripping down the steps. He stepped into the fresh air and looked up. "What the...," he muttered. There was nothing but clear sky and a rising sun. The smell rose as the goo dripped down the steps. He climbed to the dais and saw nothing. Looking down, he decided there was one giant bird or lizard hiding somewhere near and he must be more alert.

His packed gear was stored under the dais; he wouldn't need most of the stuff down below. He had his gun, knife and a net that would allow him to collect and eat. He could climb several steps and sleep safely at night.

Reaching the ground, Terry foraged for food and ate his fill of fruits and vegetables. He made his way to the edge of the jungle, there had to be a source of fresh water nearby. He quietly moved into the undergrowth and listened, moving five steps and then stopping and listening for the sound of water flowing over rocks.

It was a good morning, He found the spring after about two hours. He didn't hear it; he stepped in it. The water soaked through his boots. He breathed a sigh of relief and quenched his thirst, filled his canteens and made his way back toward the temple. Following the stream, he marked a spot near the temple that would allow him to fill his canteens without having to venture into the jungle.

Fed and hydrated, he began to search the ground-level buildings. There were various artifacts, bowls, knives, toys and other treasures, but nothing he considered of value. Night fell. He slept in one of the buildings.

With dawn's arrival, Terry checked his traps and retrieved several small animals. It was food fit for a king; after all, he was the king of the temple. He loaded his pack with fruits and other edibles and began climbing the stairs.

He chose the other side of the temple. Always checking for a door or passageway that would give him access, he began walking around the ledge to the next set of steps, hoping to see something, anything that would gain him entry to the treasure.

Halfway to the top, he rounded one of the corners and was surprised to see Mic sitting on the step. "Hello, boss. I see you found your temple."

He smiled, happy to see a friend. "Am I glad to see you!" He sat by Mic and offered him fresh water. "I've been here three days, stumbled on it by accident on the hill, up there." He pointed.

"Find anything good, boss?" Mic asked.

"Fresh water, fresh meat and a garden that's out of this world," he said with excitement. "But if you are talking about treasure, a jeweled box or anything of value, not a thing. I've searched above and below and have been looking for anything that would let me into a treasure room. It just isn't here. This is either the wrong temple, or the whole legend is just that, a legend."

"You got your map and notes, boss?" Mic asked. "Let me take a look." He studied the last of the pages and the sketches. He scanned the jungle and looked over his shoulders at the temple. After several hours, Mic stood and stretched. He continued to study the pages and the temple as he began climbing a wall.

At last, he stopped and studied the wall. "Help me push, boss."

The two men pushed; the stone moved inward, just enough to allow them to enter the temple.

"How'd you know?" he asked.

"Didn't. I sat in the middle so nothing could sneak up on me; snakes get pretty big out here. Reading your notes, I took a guess as to our height. According to your sketches, there's a door like this on each side."

The torch was old, dry and lit with the first spark. The two men followed a hallway into the temple. Terry's excitement grew, noting the drawings on the wall depicting the life and times of the Aztecs. Mic continued his pace, lighting the way. Terry followed at his own pace as he scanned the history of this ancient race.

By the time Terry caught up, he found himself inside a chamber filled with treasures beyond his imagination. The priest's headdress sat like new in a corner. Around him were gold statues of various ancient gods, the priest's tools of trade a variety of boxes, all jeweled, all valuable.

He studied the boxes. "Find the one, boss?" Mic asked. "You could open them all until you find the power to control the world. But that will take a long time."

He studied the boxes on the table and along the walls. They were ageless, representing the reign of the Aztecs. Carefully, he picked up a box. It was about three inches thick, two feet long, covered in various jewels, the cheapest being diamonds. There were engravings on the box.

"This one," he whispered. "This is the one."

Mic was busy examining the walls. "Hey, boss," he yelled, "I found a way up."

He rushed to the far corner of the room. He grinned from ear to ear and began climbing the steps. As he neared the top step, all he could see was a wall made of solid rock with no handle or hinge. He reached the top step and it sank. The wall began to rise until he found himself standing inside one of the columns that held the dais.

He stepped into the anti-chamber, and things went black.

His eyes opened; the pain in the back of his head reached his eyes by traveling through his brain. He tried to move but found himself tied to something. The sun was rising.

"Hurts like hell, doesn't it, boss?" Mic said. He released a lever from under the dais, allowing it to slide upright. He looked out toward the rising sun. There were natives in the garden; hundreds of people standing, looking up. He heard their cheers as they saw him.

"You're their hero, boss," Mic commented as he walked into his line of sight. Mic was wearing the priest's headdress and robe, "The name is Mictlantechupi, Mic just saves time. Welcome to my world. You are about to enter Mictlan, our ninth level of the underworld.

"Our great empire still lives. We are the Altec, a race over two thousand years older than the Aztec, Inca's or other races that followed us. We now live in the shadows as we protect our heritage," Mic said as he raised his arms to the crowd below.

The sounds of chanting reached his ears. One word… Quetzalcoatl.

Terry was returned to the prone position. A second man joined Mic, carrying the jeweled box. "You were right." This box rules the world, our world. This knife brings peace to my people and protects us from the outside."

With the showmanship of a Shakespearian actor, Mic played to his audience below as he opened the box's lid and removed a gold-handled dagger.

"Let me tell you what's about to happen. I am going to take this dagger and open your chest. You will remain alive and you will scream as you have never screamed before. I will rip your sternum from your chest and pry apart portions of your ribs. You will continue to scream even though your throat will be as raw as the open wound. You will be positioned and the great Quetzalcoatl will take you to the underworld," Mic exclaimed with excitement showing in his eyes. "No need to worry, I know what to do. In the outside world, I am a surgeon. There will be a lot of pain, but very little blood."

Mic began chanting. He leaned over, placing the tip of the flint-bladed knife on the skin of his sacrifice. The tip penetrated the skin just below the neck. He slid the razor-sharp edge across the chest. Terry screamed.

"Yes…scream, scream as though your last breath is in defiance of what is happening to you." His tormentor bellowed. The natives called upon the name of their winged god.

Mic continued to filet and carve Terry's chest until the skin and muscle was peeled away. The sacrifice continued screaming, even though his throat was a single dry, raw nerve. Mic smiled. "Hang in there, Terry. The sternum is next."

The blade slipped under the cartilage and severed the ribs from the sternum. "The pain is fantastic isn't it, boss? The pain must make you feel so alive at this moment. But don't worry, there's more."

Mic reached down and ripped the sternum from Terry's body. Holding it over his head, blood dripped onto Terry's face, bringing a new round of screams from the tortured man.

"Now it comes, your great sacrifice that allows me to rule the world. Do you know what it takes to rule a world? You win the hearts and minds of the people. It's simple; with your heart, I gain their minds," he said as he spread his arms out to the natives below. "Your sacrifice will keep the indigenous peoples of Mesoamerica's' secrets for another ten years. You saved one of my people from the claws of Quetzalcoatl. Thank you."

The dais began to rise. Terrified, Terry lay wide-eyed and staring at the sky, praying for all the pain to end. A shadow crossed over his face. His eyes followed the circling image. Somewhere, he knew what dropped the load of slime on the temple steps. If he hadn't been screaming, he would have laughed.

In the blink of an eye, the creature dove for the dais and seemed to float above him. The natives screamed in victory as a claw reached out, snatched Terry's heart and then rose back into the sky. The flapping of the wings dislodged a couple of feathers.

Terry continued to scream for several minutes before collapsing. Mic cut the cords holding him to the dais. The two assistants picked up the body and tossed it down the steps. At the foot, the sacrificial bonfire was already in flames, awaiting its prize.

Mic turned and stepped through the hidden door. Smiling, he descended the steps and prepared to secure the temple and return to civilization. He needed to locate a new adventurer willing to take the time to learn the Aztec secrets and receive the rewards from the older Altec nation. He would find an adventurer seeking great riches and power as they searched for the box that would allow them to rule the world.

High above, the giant bird settled into its nest. It fed pieces of the heart to small creatures lying under their mother's body. Soon, they too would take to the sky and, someday, they would help return the Altec people to their proper place in the world.

ABOUT THE AUTHOR

John W. Smith was born in East St. Louis, Illinois and reared in the Metro East. His love for comics introduced him to reading. In the third grade, he discovered "real books." He fell in love with science-fiction and horror. He devoured book after book about creatures of the night and other monsters (human and otherwise). His reading sparked an interest in writing.

He received his degree in journalism and honed his abilities in public affairs with the U.S. Air Force. Retiring in 1992, he bought a Harley and began promoting motorcycle freedom and safety through a variety of California magazines, as well as national and international publications.

In civilian life, he worked for the *Bakersfield Californian* newspaper in advertising. This taught him the importance of editing to reduce word count, yet carry a punch in your sentences.

He has started several "Great American Novels," but he enjoys writing short stories. He is attempting to create novel-length works, but it takes time as he writes each chapter as though it were a continuing short story.

John has contributed stories to *Words, An Anthology of Short Stories* (2011). He published his first book of short stories entitled *Nightmares of a Madman* (2013). John edited and coordinated *A Dark and Stormy Night, an* anthology (2014). His short stories, *Spirit Dagger, Colonial Scum* and *Hungry Things* are available in electronic format at Kindle, SmashWords.com and other sites.

In addition, John is currently working on two novels that have not been titled at this time. The first is a romance novel for his mother and the second is dark fiction.

Contact John through his website at:
www.johnwsmithauthor.com
or email
writerphotographer1946@gmail.com

CPSIA information can be obtained
at www.ICGtesting.com
Printed in the USA
FFOW03n0400260117
31692FF